Rea
Reasoner, James.
Tie a black ribbon

$ 21.95

1st ed.

Tie a Black Ribbon

Other Five Star titles
by Livia J. Washburn:

Wild Night

Tie a Black Ribbon

James Reasoner
and Livia J. Washburn

Five Star
Unity, Maine

Five Star Mystery Series.

Published in conjunction with Tekno Books and Ed Gorman.

March 2000

First Edition

Cover photograph courtesy of Barb Littlefield.

The text of this edition is unabridged.

Set in 11 pt. Plantin by Al Chase.

Printed in the United States on permanent paper.

Library of Congress Cataloging-in-Publication Data
Reasoner, James.
   Tie a black ribbon / by James Reasoner &
Livia J. Washburn. — 1st ed.
     p.   cm.
   ISBN 0-7862-2362-6 (hc : alk. paper)
   I. Washburn, Livia J. II. Title.
PS3568.E2685 T54 2000
813´.54—dc21   99-056407

For Shayna and Joanna,

and their little dog, too.

Chapter One

Skeeter was singing "Jose Cuervo, You Are a Friend of Mine" under her breath as she walked into the Horsehead Bar and Grill. She looked across the room and nodded to Jasper, a grin on her face. He watched her as she made her way toward him. The club was already crowded, even though it was only eight o'clock on a Thursday night.

"You look mighty happy, gal," Jasper said as she reached the bar and leaned her elbows on it. He drew a beer, passed it across the hardwood to a customer, and turned back to Skeeter. "Somethin' good happen?"

"Shoot, something good's always happening—to somebody, somewhere," she replied.

"Man could say the same about somethin' bad."

Skeeter shrugged. "Maybe you're right. Bring on the iced tea."

He had it ready for her, as usual. Taking the pitcher out of a little refrigerator under the bar, he poured a full tumbler and handed it to her. Iced tea was all she would drink while she was working, and she'd go through a couple of pitchers between now and two o'clock in the morning. The first pitcher would be the regular stuff, the second decaffeinated so that she could get to sleep before dawn—if she was lucky.

She turned around, putting her back to the bar, and sipped the tea. Her green eyes scanned the room, looking for any signs of trouble. Being head of security for the Horsehead—meaning she was a bouncer and a damn good one—required her to head off problems before they got se-

7

rious and required things like beer bottles to the skull, fists to the belly, and knees in the groin.

The Horsehead was no Billy Bob's, which was down the street in Fort Worth's historic Stockyards area, but it was a good-sized nightclub with a sprawling main room and several smaller rooms that could be rented for private parties. The bar stretched along the left side of the main room and was elevated slightly. A couple of plank steps led up to the wooden deck in front of the bar. The garish glow from several neon beer signs washed over the hardwood. There was a long mirror over the back bar, and above the mirror was the horse skull that gave the place its name.

On the other wall, toward the back, was a bandstand with a dance floor between it and the bar. A split-rail fence separated the dance floor from the deck. The front part of the room was filled with heavy wooden tables, and there were a few booths along that section of the right-hand wall. The lighting was subdued, most of it coming from fixtures made to look like old-fashioned kerosene lanterns. A magnificent spread of longhorns decorated the wall above the entrance doors. There was even sawdust on the floors.

But no plastic cactus. You had to draw the line somewhere, Jasper always said.

The clientele was a mixture: well-to-do young people from the southwest side of town, ropers from the north side, tourists wanting to find some evidence that Fort Worth was still "The City Where the West Begins" despite all the fancy glass skyscrapers downtown, drunks who cared only that the Horsehead served liquor, and even a few real cowboys. The genuine article . . . Skeeter always thought of them that way. Most of the time she liked these folks and got along well with the majority of them.

The buzz of conversation and laughter filled the room.

Music from a jukebox in the corner added to the clamor. On Friday and Saturday nights, Jasper usually had a live band booked to play, but during the rest of the week, the jukebox provided tunes for dancing. The 'box wouldn't fall silent until the place closed at two.

Two bartenders besides Jasper handled most of the load, leaving the Horsehead's owner free to talk to Skeeter over the strains of a George Strait song. "Everything's been pretty quiet," he said. "Got a hunch we're in for a peaceful evening."

Skeeter looked back over her shoulder and frowned. Jasper Lowe's hunches were notorious for being wrong. About the only hunch that had worked out well for Jasper was opening this saloon, she mused. It had been a solid moneymaker for him.

She didn't know how old Jasper was. Hard to tell when a man was all whipcord and leather like that. But from the lines on his face and the gray in his hair and drooping moustache, she would have said fifty or so. He knew how to keep his mouth shut and listen to the customers' troubles, and he made a heck of a drink.

"I'll remember how peaceful you told me it was going to be when I have to clout some ol' boy over the head," she told him. "Or maybe you just meant that nobody was going to get killed tonight."

Jasper just grinned.

Skeeter shook her head. Time to drift around the room, size things up a little.

There were eyes following her as she moved along the edge of the dance floor, past a few boot-scootin' couples. She was used to men watching her, had been ever since she was twelve years old and started shooting up and out and got to looking like a woman. She had developed early, according to her mama, and she didn't stop for quite a while. Even though she was big—a shade under six feet and a shade over a hundred and fifty pounds—she was well-proportioned. The thick red hair, worn long and free, made her look younger than her thirty-three years. She wore comfortable old boots, jeans that were tight but not so much so that she couldn't move around in a hurry if she needed to, a long-sleeved white Western shirt with pearl snaps, and a fringed leather vest decorated with conchos. The wide, brown leather belt around her waist was fastened by a large silver buckle with a longhorn on it, and *SKEETER* was written on the back. The first time she had looked at herself in the mirror while she was wearing a getup like this, she had muttered, "Dale Evans lives."

That was a long time ago, and she couldn't imagine being comfortable any other way now.

Working in the bar had given her the knack of being able to pick up conversations through the constant blare of music. As she passed a table full of college boys from TCU or UTA, some who looked a little familiar, she heard one of them say, "Hey! Who's that?"

"Don't waste your time, Phil. She works here."

"She's a waitress?"

A couple of the other young men laughed. "Bouncer," one of them said.

"A *girl?*"

"Just cause some trouble and watch how quick she stops it."

"No foolin'?"

"Anyway," one of the others said, "she's a dyke."

"With a body like that? What a waste!"

Skeeter looked back over her shoulder, caught the eye of the boy who had asked the others about her, smiled sweetly, and kissed the air at him. Then she moved on, leaving him staring.

People around the Horsehead, employees and regular customers alike, had been wondering about her sexual preferences for quite a while. She never dated any of the men who came on to her. Most of the regulars had her pegged as a lesbian, especially since she'd brought Rita in with her one night and introduced her as her roommate. Skeeter didn't care; rumors like that just made her job easier because she didn't have to fend off as many drunken passes that way. The few men she went out with, she had met away from both of her jobs.

By the time she'd made a circuit of the room, said hello to a few customers, and reached the bar again, she had polished off the first glass of iced tea. Jasper gave her a refill, then said, "You're still grinnin' like a possum. Goin' to tell me about it or not?"

"Not," Skeeter said. It was none of Jasper Lowe's business that she had finally gotten another case that would take her out of the office and away from that damned telephone. Being a private investigator, she thought, had probably been a lot more fun back in the era when legwork involved human legs, rather than phones and computers.

Maybe the good ol' days could actually come back . . .

Chapter Two

The glass door that led into the suite of offices had a sign painted on it that read *THE HALLAM AGENCY* and gave the phone numbers. Inside was a small reception area that looked more like the waiting room of a doctor's office than the entrance to a private detective agency. The reception area led into a hallway with two doors. The second door opened into the large office of Lars Gilford, the branch manager. Behind the first door was the much smaller office shared by Skeeter and the other part-timer, a pre-law student at UTA named Tommy Fuller, who was every bit as clean-cut as his name sounded.

Skeeter was alone late that afternoon, updating some of the files in the computer, when she heard the muted bell that announced someone had come into the reception area. With a couple of keystrokes, she started saving the file, then stood up and stepped into the hall.

A woman who was half a dozen years older than Skeeter, maybe a little more, stood in the reception area, peering down the corridor through stylish glasses. She smiled at Skeeter, pushed back a strand of brunette hair that had strayed in front of her left eye, and said, "Hello. I'm looking for a detective."

Skeeter returned the smile. "Any detective in particular?"

The woman looked a little hesitant. She said, "This *is* a detective agency, isn't it?"

"One of the best in the country," Skeeter assured her. "Come on back to the office."

She wasn't wearing the same sort of clothes she wore at the

Horsehead, but she supposed she didn't look like any kind of executive, either. She had on a dark green short-sleeved pullover and khaki pants. Standing to one side to let the potential client enter first—politeness never hurt anyone, Mama always said—Skeeter went on, "The manager is out of the office right now, but I'd be glad to help you. I'm Cassandra Barlow."

"Tracy Roberts," the woman introduced herself as she sat down and Skeeter went behind the desk again. "Are you a private detective?"

"Yes, ma'am, fully licensed and bonded by the State of Texas. I'd be glad to show you—"

Tracy Roberts shook her head. "No, I'm sorry, that's not necessary. I was just a little surprised . . . Well, you know, even in this day and age . . ."

"Yes, ma'am, I understand." All too well sometimes, Skeeter thought. She had two jobs, and neither of them was what folks normally thought of as a woman's line of work. She pushed the monitor screen to one side so that it wouldn't be a distraction as she looked across the desk at Tracy Roberts. "Now, what can the Hallam Agency do for you?"

"I want you to find a dog for me."

A missing pet case. Skeeter tried not to sigh. She had heard of such things, of course. Everybody in the detective business had. But she had considered them sort of on the same level with other urban myths, like alligators in the sewers and giant Mexican rats that tourists brought home with them thinking the varmints were dogs. Tracy Roberts appeared to be completely serious.

"You want us to find a dog," Skeeter said slowly. "And return it to you when we do, I assume."

"God, no." Tracy Robert's eyes widened in surprise. "I'd rather you shot the vicious beast in the head." She sighed.

"But I don't suppose I could hire a reputable agency to do something like that."

Now it was Skeeter's turn to be surprised by the hatred she had heard in Tracy Robert's voice. Finally, she said, "No, I don't believe you could. I guess this isn't your dog you're talking about."

"No, thank goodness. I'd never have such a brute. The animal belongs to a man named Frank Hobson."

"Is he a friend of yours?" A woman might want to help her boyfriend find his lost dog, even if she didn't like the animal herself, Skeeter thought.

Tracy Roberts put a stop to that line of thought. "No, he's not a friend. He and his wife used to live down the street from me. He and Raider are a good match for each other."

"Raider?"

"The dog I want you to find."

"Did he run away from home?"

"No, the Hobsons took him with them when they moved." Tracy Roberts closed her eyes and lifted her hand to her forehead. After massaging it with her fingertips for a moment, she looked up and said, "I'm not making much sense, am I?"

Skeeter had been thinking that very thing, even though she wouldn't say so to a client, at least not this early on. She suggested, "Maybe if you just went back and started at the beginning . . ."

"Of course. I live in Arlington Heights." She gave the address, and Skeeter made a note of it on a legal pad. "Like I told you, this man Hobson and his wife lived down the street from me. He had Raider in his back yard."

"What kind of dog are we talking about?"

"A pit bull."

Somehow that answer didn't surprise Skeeter. "Do the Hobsons have any children?"

Tracy Roberts shook her head. "Just Raider. The way Frank Hobson loves that dog, you'd think it was a child."

"And you said the Hobsons moved?"

"Yes, after the trouble this last time."

"Trouble with the dog?"

"He bit my nephew." Tracy Roberts' hands clenched tightly on her purse, and her breathing began to come a little faster with remembered fear and anger. "It took over a hundred stitches in Joey's face to close up the wounds. Can you imagine what an ordeal that was for an eight-year-old?"

Skeeter nodded and said, "I'm sorry." She meant it. Her son Doug was almost eight, and she knew how she'd feel if something like that ever happened to him.

"Joey and his mother—my sister Beth—were visiting me, and Joey went out into the front yard to play. I didn't think . . . Even though Raider had gotten loose and bitten several people before, I never expected . . . My own children are all older, and I guess I got out of practice at worrying about such things." Tracy Roberts smiled weakly. "I haven't had to warn my children about petting strange animals for years."

Now that the woman had mentioned more of the details, Skeeter recalled reading newspaper stories about the incident. She had no idea what had become of the dog. Under the circumstances, she would have assumed that it would be destroyed.

When she said as much, Tracy Roberts nodded vehemently. "That's what everyone thought would happen. But Frank Hobson got a lawyer and went to court, and he was able to work out an arrangement so that he could keep Raider. He had to move the dog out of Tarrant County, otherwise Raider would have been destroyed as a public menace. Like I said, he's bitten several people besides my nephew, although the attack on Joey was the worst."

Skeeter leaned back in her chair and thought about how to phrase her next question. After a moment, she said, "Is it possible that your nephew might have unintentionally frightened or hurt the dog?"

"Not at all. There were quite a few witnesses. Joey was bouncing a basketball off the front wall of my house when Raider came running down the street. He ran into my yard and jumped on Joey for no reason. Beth and I heard him screaming and ran outside right away, of course. I don't know what we would have done if a couple of men from the neighborhood hadn't been out working in their yards. It was a Sunday afternoon, you know."

Skeeter hadn't, but she made a mental note of it.

"One of them had a shovel, and he hit Raider in the head with it until the dog let go of Joey. The other man grabbed Joey and carried him away from the dog. Raider was about to turn on them when Frank Hobson showed up. He'd slipped out the gate while Frank was going in." Tracy Roberts' voice trembled slightly as she went on, "We called 911. Joey was bleeding so badly, we thought he was dead. When the paramedics arrived, they said he was in shock."

"How is he now?"

"Better. Physically, at least, although he does have some awful scars. When he's older, the doctors will do some cosmetic surgery and see if they can improve his looks. Emotionally . . . well, his schoolwork suffered, and he has nightmares several times a week. Bad nightmares, the kind that make him wake up screaming."

"I'm really sorry, Mrs. Roberts. It sounds like an awful experience. What did the police do when they got there?"

"Well, the animal control people came, of course. They wanted to take Raider with them. I didn't see much of this, Beth and I were too concerned with Joey. But I heard about it later from the neighbors. Frank wasn't going to let them take Raider. He accused them of wanting to kill the dog. They almost came to blows before the police officers on the scene told Frank they'd arrest him, too, if he didn't settle down. Laurie had come down the street by then, too, and she was finally able to calm him down."

"Laurie?"

"Frank's wife."

"What happened with the dog?" Skeeter asked. "Surely they quarantined it in case of rabies?"

"Yes. Considering what had happened, the Public Health Department wanted to go ahead and destroy the animal and send the head to Austin for rabies tests. But Frank's lawyer got a court order immediately to prevent them from doing that. Even though Frank had records on Raider's vaccinations, they kept the dog quarantined. Of course, Raider didn't have rabies. He's just vicious, like all of those pit bulls."

Skeeter tended to agree with her generalization. She knew people who swore that pit bulls were as gentle as any other breed of dog when they were treated right, but she'd never seen any evidence of it.

Tracy Roberts sighed. "Anyway, once it was certain Raider didn't have rabies, Frank's lawyer talked to the District Attorney and worked out an agreement."

"The one stating that Raider couldn't live in Tarrant County?"

"Exactly. The court order applied only to the dog itself, but it didn't surprise me when Frank up and moved, too, rather than give Raider away or sell him. He'd rather uproot Laurie than be separated from that dog."

Skeeter thought Tracy Roberts sounded like she was sorry for Laurie Hobson, probably with good reason. Frank didn't exactly sound like any sort of prize.

"That's all the legal action that was taken?"

Nodding, Tracy Roberts said, "We didn't like it, but there was nothing we could do."

"You could sue Frank Hobson," Skeeter pointed out. Generally, she was uncomfortable with the way people filed lawsuits at the slightest excuse, but in this case, it might be justified.

"No. He paid for Joey's medical bills, or at least his lawyer did. When the man brought the check, he had a paper for Beth to sign. It was a waiver, of course. Besides, we don't have the money for any sort of legal battle. I'm a widow, and Beth is divorced. Both of us are secretaries. Neither of us make the kind of money you need to hire lawyers and file lawsuits."

Skeeter felt a little surge of anger. Too many people thought they could buy their way out of anything—and too often, they were right.

"So, if that's where things stand now, I'm not sure why you want to hire the agency—"

"I don't trust Frank Hobson." Tracy Roberts' voice was sharp. "It would be just like him to move out of the county for a little while, then come right back." She leaned forward. "I want to be sure that dog is as far away as possible. I want to be able to tell my nephew that Raider will never bother him again."

Under the circumstances, that sounded like a reasonable goal, Skeeter thought. "Do you know where the Hobsons went when they moved?"

"No. They just packed up and left."

"What are you going to do if we find out Raider's back in the county? Or still here, for that matter?"

"I'm going to report it to the authorities. And this time I'll pursue it until they do something about that animal. You *are* going to take this case, aren't you, Ms. Barlow?"

Skeeter frowned. She wanted to say yes, but Lars Gilford was supposed to make the final call on such things. Besides, if Tracy Roberts didn't have enough money to hire a lawyer, would she be able to pay the agency's fees?

"Tell you what," she said after a moment. "We'll go ahead and fill out the contracts, but they won't be official until my boss looks them over and signs them. He won't be in until tomorrow morning. But I'll go ahead and make a few phone calls this afternoon and see what I can find out."

"Thank you," Tracy Roberts said, and Skeeter could hear the relief in the woman's voice. "I suppose you'll need a check . . ."

"Better wait until Mr. Gilford okays everything. Our rates are three hundred dollars a day plus expenses, and we usually ask for a two thousand dollar retainer—" Skeeter hurried on as she saw the stricken expression starting to appear on the other woman's face. "—but I imagine we can waive the retainer in this case. It shouldn't take more than a day or two to turn up the dog. Can you handle that?"

Tracy Roberts nodded. "Yes, I have seven hundred and fifty dollars set aside for this. I know you're probably used to much bigger cases—"

"Honey, if it'll get me off my butt and out of this office, I'm all for it." The words came out of Skeeter's mouth before she thought, and for a second she thought Tracy Roberts might be offended, but then the other woman broke into a grin. That was the first genuine expression of pleasure Skeeter had seen on her face since she walked into the place.

"I think I'm glad I came to see you, Ms. Barlow," she said.

Skeeter returned the grin. "So am I."

★ ★ ★ ★ ★

As she had promised Tracy Roberts, she made some phone calls after the woman left, starting with Directory Assistance for Tarrant County. They had no listing for a Frank Hobson, new or old, at least not under that name. She tried Parker County, the next one to the west, then worked her way in a circle: Wise, Denton, Dallas, Ellis, Johnson, and Hood Counties. If the Hobsons had moved farther away than that, then Raider was no longer a threat to anybody in the Fort Worth area. She found a Frank Hobson in Denton County and another in Hood County. The one in Hood County insisted he'd never owned a pit bull in his life or heard of Tracy Roberts and her nephew; the number in Denton County didn't answer.

The calls didn't really tell her that much. The Hobsons might not have a phone wherever they had moved after leaving Arlington Heights, or the number might be unlisted. Skeeter wasn't worried. There were plenty of other ways to trace people, but it had made sense to try the easiest route first. It was too late to head downtown to the county courthouse, so she put the Roberts contract on Lars Gilford's desk along with a note, then headed back to her house to shower and change before going to the Horsehead.

She was still leaning on the bar, thinking about what had happened that afternoon, when she heard Jasper say, "Uh-oh."

Skeeter looked around in a hurry, mentally kicking herself for letting her mind wander that way. She asked, "Trouble?"

Jasper nodded toward one of the tables.

Two couples were sitting there, and the men were arguing. They were in their forties, Skeeter judged, both of them a little thick in the belly. Their hats were shoved back on their heads, and they were jawing at each other pretty good. The women were looking on with resigned, almost bored expressions on their faces.

"I'll handle it," Skeeter told Jasper.

"Reckon you'll need help? Chuckie's gone to the back to bring up another keg of beer."

Chuckie had been a reserve linebacker on the '92 TCU Horned Frogs, and now he worked as a combination bartender/bouncer/general flunky for Jasper. Skeeter didn't think this little problem was going to amount to much, so she shook her head and said, "Nah, I'll be all right."

She started across the room toward the table where the men were arguing. Reba McIntire was singing on the jukebox, and the couples on the floor were slow-dancing. Skeeter weaved around a few tables. One of the men was shaking his finger in the other's face. She could hear them shouting at each other.

"Here now, boys," Skeeter said brightly as she came up beside them. "What's the trouble?"

They stopped arguing, and both of them looked at her in surprise. "Who the hell are you, lady?" one of them asked.

"I work here, and it looked like you gents were havin' a little problem."

"Only problem we got is that the pitcher's empty," the other one growled. "Bring us another."

"Well, now, I'd be glad to . . . if you and your buddy would stop hollerin'. You don't want to disturb folks who've come here for a good time."

One of the women spoke up. "This *is* their idea of a good time."

The other woman added, "They do this at least once a month. Come out to a club, start arguin' about some damn fool thing, then whale the tar out of each other. Been doin' it for years."

21

"Then I'm truly sorry to interrupt your routine, fellas, but there's really not supposed to be any fightin' in here. Tell you what—if you'll shake hands and call a truce, I'll bring you that pitcher of beer you wanted. How 'bout it?"

One of the men rubbed his jaw. "Well . . . why not?" He extended his hand across the table. "I'll shake if you will, Bobby."

"Sure, Fred."

The only problem was that as soon as their hands clasped, Fred jerked Bobby forward over the table and smashed his other fist into Bobby's face.

Skeeter saw it coming, but not in time to stop it. She moved. Fred was off-balance, leaning forward over the table, so she kicked his chair out from under him. He spilled to the floor, but he still had hold of Bobby's hand, so he dragged the other man with him. The table went over with a crash. Customers at the surrounding tables scooted their chairs out of the way and went back to their drinking. The record in the jukebox had changed to an old Alabama song that had the dancers moving faster again. Skeeter leaned over and grabbed the men's collars, trying to drag them apart as they started to roll around and wrestle with each other in the sawdust. A spitting, hissing weight landed on Skeeter's back.

The first rule of bar fights, and she had forgotten it: *watch the women—they're sneakier.* Skeeter drove an elbow back into the belly of the woman who was reaching around and clawing at her face, knocking her off into the floor. The other one was coming at her, swinging a chair.

"No redheaded slut's gonna do that to Fred!" she yelled.

Skeeter bent at the waist, letting the chair go over her head, and snapped a side kick that would have had her martial arts instructor screaming at her about how sloppy she was. It got the job done, thudding into the woman's solar plexus and knocking her on her rump.

About that time, Jasper and Chuckie showed up, grabbed the two men, and hustled them toward the door. The women got up, moaning and complaining, and followed. As Jasper came back from throwing all four of them out of the place, Skeeter pushed her hair out of her face, grinned at him, and said, "Nice peaceful night, huh?"

Jasper spread his hands and shrugged. "Hey. Nobody got killed."

Chapter Three

Around ten the next morning, Skeeter pointed her blue Ford pickup toward downtown Fort Worth. Lars hadn't called to tell her that the agency wasn't taking the Roberts case, so she forged ahead.

Cursing the torn-up downtown streets—every time she came down here, one more street was filled with bulldozers, piles of gravel, and guys in hard hats standing around looking at God knows what in the sky—she circled for fifteen minutes looking for a parking place within reasonable walking distance of the courthouse. After that, she gave up, drove down to the Tandy parking lot, and rode the little subway car to the shopping center on the edge of downtown. From there it was only a three-block walk to the massive old stone courthouse.

Half an hour in the county clerk's office confirmed everything that Tracy Roberts had told her. An agreement had been worked out between Frank Hobson, the District Attorney, and one of the District Court judges. Raider was to be removed from Tarrant County for a period of not less than two years, and if the order was not complied with, Frank Hobson would be charged with contempt of court and the dog would be destroyed. Hobson had been given thirty days to make the necessary arrangements and report the dog's whereabouts to the court clerk. Failing that, a bench warrant would be issued for him. Skeeter didn't find any record of such a warrant, so she assumed Hobson had gone along with the deal.

Which didn't mean he couldn't have moved back into the

county after satisfying the initial terms of the judgment. Skeeter headed upstairs to the courtrooms and the judges' offices.

She was lucky. Court wasn't in session at the moment, and the clerk she needed to see was in his office.

"Hobson? The name sounds vaguely familiar, but with all the cases we have to process . . . As a private investigator, you should know better than most people how overworked the judicial system is, Ms. Barlow."

The clerk was in his forties, looked like he spent his days off on the racquetball court, and didn't seem the type to be a prissy little bureaucrat. In fact, when she'd first walked into the office, Skeeter had found herself wondering if he was married. Now, after talking to him for only a couple of minutes, she just wanted to find out what she needed to know and then get out of there.

"I'm sorry to bother you, Mr. Gustafson," she said again, having prefaced her questions with the same statement. "If you could just look up that information for me, I'll get right out of your hair, I promise."

The clerk grunted, opened the middle drawer of his metal desk, and took out a pair of glasses. He settled them on the tip of his nose like an old lady and turned toward his computer, tilting his head back so that he could see through the lenses. His fingers tapped the keys for a moment; he hesitated, waiting for something to come up on the screen, then typed some more.

"There you are," he said when he paused this time. He read off an address out of the Boyd post office, northwest of Fort Worth in Wise County. Skeeter wrote it down quickly in her notebook. Gustafson went on, "That's where this man Hobson is supposed to be living. At any rate, that's the address he reported to the District Attorney's office. I think you're wasting your time and your client's money, Ms. Barlow."

"Could be," Skeeter admitted. "I reckon peace of mind's worth something, nonetheless."

"Indeed." Gustafson hit a key and cleared the screen. "Now, was there anything else you needed?"

"Nope, that'll do it. I appreciate it. You have a good day, hear?"

Gustafson grunted again, and Skeeter didn't bother to smile at him before she left the office. She'd just be wasting the effort, she thought.

The sun was bright in her face as she emerged from the building and started down the long, steep flight of steps that led to the sidewalk. A lot of people were coming and going. The north end of downtown stayed busy. The courthouse and the combination sheriff's department/jail next door brought a great deal of traffic to the surrounding blocks, which were filled with lawyers' offices and bail bondsmen. For a town that prided itself on its friendliness, Fort Worth had more than its share of crime.

The Stockyards were only a couple of miles away, across the river and out North Main Street, but that couple of miles made a world of difference. The area might be a tourist trap, but Skeeter felt comfortable there. She couldn't say the same about downtown. Heck, the way they kept throwing new buildings up, you never knew when a crane or a girder might fall on you. Hadn't happened to anybody yet—but it *could,* she thought.

The Hallam Agency was located on the third floor of a ten-story office building on the West Freeway, about halfway between Skeeter's house and downtown. Tommy Fuller was in the reception area making a fresh pot of coffee when Skeeter came into the office a few minutes before one.

"Hi," he said, barely glancing up. He was tall and skinny, with blond hair that stuck up naturally. Skeeter always thought he looked like he should be hanging out at the mall or going to a prom or something, even though he was twenty-three years old. He was sharp as all get out and in Skeeter's estimation could probably make a hell of a P.I. someday, if he had wanted to. He was just getting some practical experience, he claimed, before he went on to law school.

"Hi. Lars get back?"

"He's in his office." Tommy didn't ask if she wanted any coffee, knowing quite well that she didn't drink the stuff.

She went down the hall to Lars Gilford's office. She knocked and opened the door when he called, "Come in."

As usual, he didn't look busy, even though there were a few papers on the desk in front of him. He got everything done, but Skeeter didn't know when. She'd never seen him actually working.

"How was Austin?" she asked as she sat down in the client's chair in front of the big desk. He had gone down to the state capital the day before to testify in a court case in which the agency had been hired by the plaintiff.

He shrugged his narrow shoulders. "Fine," he said. Skeeter didn't expect much more of an answer than that. Lars Gilford was reserved to the point of almost disappearing at times. His pale hair, fair skin, and first name had come from his Scandinavian mother. Skeeter didn't particularly like him, but she had to admit that he did a good job running the place. Only rarely was he summoned to the home office in Los Angeles to face Elizabeth Hallam, the founder of the agency.

She glanced at the documents on the desktop and spotted the Roberts contract. Her note was still clipped to the form.

Pointing at it, she said, "Did you have a chance to look that over?"

"Yes, I did. I read it this morning." Gilford's bushy eyebrows drew down. "I take it you've already begun an investigation into the matter?"

Skeeter smiled. "I guess you know me pretty well, Lars. I didn't think it would hurt to poke around a mite."

"And?"

"And as far as I can tell, Frank Hobson and Raider are living up close to Boyd. That's across the county line in Wise County."

"I know. Would you like to drive up there this afternoon and confirm that information?"

"I was hoping to, yes."

Gilford nodded. "Very well. I'll be here to handle anything that comes up, and since you've already put in some time on the case, we should go ahead and wrap it up so that we can justifiably charge the lady for a day's work. Do you think you'll be back by six?"

Skeeter was a little surprised by his quick agreement. She hadn't even had to argue about anything. The trip to Austin must have gone better than Lars was willing to admit. Skeeter said, "Ought to be back well before then."

Gilford flipped the contract over to the second page and scrawled his signature. "There. Now everything is official."

She stood up and said, "Thanks."

Gilford didn't look up as she walked out.

He was a cold fish, but that was all right. At least he wasn't all over her like that fella Rita worked for at the video store. If he had been Skeeter's boss, he'd wind up on the floor mighty quick, hugging his groin and calling for his mama.

She peeked in the smaller room as she passed by and saw Tommy whaling away at the keyboard. "Gonna be late for class," she warned him.

"Just a few more minutes . . . I'm on to something."

He was their resident hacker, and any time a case involved computers, it was usually Tommy who carried the ball. Skeeter could use one of the machines, of course, and so could Gilford, but neither of them possessed the flair for it that Tommy did.

She waved and went on out.

The town of Boyd consisted of four or five blocks of business development along a state highway which the farm road intersected. The post office was right on the highway, and Skeeter pulled in there and parked. She went inside the small brick building.

Two minutes of conversation with the clerk told her where to find the address she was looking for. Skeeter pretended to be a messenger with a package to deliver, a pose that never failed to work.

The wind was out of the north and getting stronger as Skeeter climbed back into the pickup and backed carefully onto the highway. The Hobson place—if indeed they still lived there—was east of town, on the highway toward Rhome. Skeeter rolled up the window as she headed in that direction. The air was too chilly now to have it open.

She grinned as she passed a sign reading AURORA. That was the little community where the flying saucer had crashed back at the turn of the century. Folks claimed it had, anyway. The alien pilot had been badly hurt in the crash, and being good Texans, the citizens of Aurora had taken him in and cared for him, despite the fact that he was little and silver and shiny. He'd died from his injuries, and he was supposed to be buried out in the little community cemetery.

None of which had anything to do with the reason she was here, she reminded herself. She watched the side of the

29

highway for the dirt road she was supposed to find.

A few minutes later, she found it, a narrow lane of hard-packed dirt that turned off to the right. She braked and swung the pickup onto it, raising a cloud of dust. Mailboxes sat on posts next to the road, and she searched for one with numbers on it. The houses along here were all old frame structures with big front yards and pastures in the back. Skeeter saw more than one dilapidated barn and chicken house behind the dwellings, too. The people who lived out here were probably below the poverty level, most of them, anyway. But she saw a few brand-new pickups, too, fresh paint jobs gleaming in the autumn sun. Here and there she spotted a satellite dish sitting next to a house badly in need of repairs.

These people might live in rundown homes, but by God, they could drive to work in a new pickup and then come home and watch TV off the satellite. She spotted a mailbox with the right numbers stenciled on it. The house was on the left, a big frame structure that was neatly painted and seemed in better repair than some of the other homes in the area. A Cadillac was parked in the one-car garage attached to the side of the house, and a pickup was parked behind it in the driveway. Skeeter pulled in behind the pickup.

As she stepped out of her vehicle and pulled her jacket on, several large dogs bounded around the corner of the house from the back of the place, barking furiously. She tensed, ready to dive back into the pickup, until she saw the expressions on the faces of the animals and the way their tails were going a mile a minute.

"Vicious brutes, ain't they?" a woman's voice called from the porch of the house. "Here! You boys leave that lady alone! Better watch out, honey, they'll pure-dee lick you to death if you're not careful."

Skeeter laughed, petted a couple of the big dogs as they

came nuzzling up to her, and started toward the house. The dogs trailed her. As she looked up at the porch, she saw an elderly woman, short and wide in a flowered print dress and a white knitted sweater. Her hair was the same color as the sweater. She wore thick glasses and leaned on a cane, but despite that, there was an air of vitality about her as she came to the edge of the porch and smiled a greeting at Skeeter. A small Chihuahua Doberman looking dog skittered around her feet, glaring at the visitor and snarling.

The old lady indicated the tiny dog with her cane. "This'un's the one you got to watch out for. He'll eat you up. Dobie, you behave yourself! What can I do for you, honey?"

Skeeter returned the grin and said, "Is this the Hobson residence?"

"No, ma'am," the woman said. "I'm Ida Lou Culbertson, and this is my place."

Skeeter frowned a little. "I was told a man named Frank Hobson lived at this address."

"He got his mail here for a little while." Dobie started to yap, a high-pitched, nerve-wracking sound, and the old woman prodded it gently with the cane. "Hush!" She looked back at Skeeter and went on, "The Hobsons rented the trailer house out back."

Skeeter hadn't noticed a mobile home in the rear of the place when she drove in, but she hadn't been looking for one. She said, "Oh, I see. But they don't live here any more?"

Ida Lou Culbertson shook her head. "Nope. Had to ask 'em to move out. You ain't a friend of theirs, are you?"

"Never met either one of them," Skeeter replied honestly.

"Good. 'Course, wouldn't't've been anything wrong with you bein' a friend of Laurie's. She was a mighty nice girl. But that Frank . . ." Ida Lou Culbertson sighed and looked grim.

"Gave you trouble, did he?"

"Him and that *dog!* Got so's I had to keep my animals penned up and make sure Dobie stayed in the house all the time. No, ma'am, I wasn't sorry to see that Raider dog go! And I don't miss Frank's friends, either."

Skeeter's only real purpose in coming here had been to see if Frank Hobson—and Raider—were still living outside of Tarrant County. But she was curious. Skeeter asked, "What can you tell me about his friends?"

Ida Lou Culbertson opened her mouth to reply, shut it suddenly, then opened it again to say, "Honey, I don't know why you're askin' all these questions or even what your name is."

Skeeter reached into her purse and brought out her wallet. Flipping it open to the copy of her license, she held the identification up toward the porch and went on, "My name is Cassandra Barlow. I'm a private investigator."

Ida Lou Culbertson's eyes widened. "You mean like Shell Scott?"

It was Skeeter's turn to be surprised. She would have expected the woman to compare her to Rockford or Magnum, somebody from TV reruns, not to a fictional P.I. from books. She said, "Well, sort of . . ."

"How about that! I read all of those books back when they first came out. My late husband collected 'em. Never thought I'd meet a real private eye." She waved at the wallet in Skeeter's hand. "Might as well put that away, I can't read print that small anymore. Come on up here on the porch and have a seat. Dobie, you get back in the house!"

Ida Lou Culbertson opened the screen door and prodded the small dog back into the house. It stood just inside, its little black nose pressed to the screen, and growled some more. Skeeter gave the door a wide berth as she stepped up onto the porch.

The old woman sat down in a metal swing suspended by chains from the porch roof and gestured for Skeeter to take a large wicker chair nearby. Skeeter settled down in it. Ida Lou Culbertson said, "Frank involved in some case you're workin' on?"

"He's involved in a case, all right, but I'm afraid I can't go into any of the details."

"Oh, I understand that, honey. Now, you wanted to know about his friends."

"If you don't mind."

"Well, Frank didn't introduce me to any of 'em, you understand. But I couldn't help but see 'em comin' and goin'. You got to drive right past the house to get to the trailer. I saw the pickups. They all had gun racks, and the men drivin' them had a hard look about 'em, if you know what I mean."

Skeeter wasn't sure she did, but she nodded.

"And then there were the big fancy cars, some of them foreign jobbies the Krauts make. The men who came in those, they looked like they sure hated gettin' dust all over their cars, but there wasn't nothin' they could do about it. Only one way back to that trailer house, you know. Anyway, they'd come in their fancy cars and their fancy suits, sometimes two or three times a week. Now I ask you, what were fellas like that doin' visitin' somebody like Frank Hobson?"

"I don't know, Mrs. Culbertson. It does sound a little funny."

The old woman sniffed. "It surely was. Made me nervous, let me tell you. I got to wonderin' if the boy was sellin' dope or something."

Skeeter asked, "Do you know where Hobson works?"

"He was out at Lockheed while he was livin' here. I suppose he still is, unless he's got fired or laid off since him and Laurie moved."

"How long have they been gone?"

"Lemme see now . . . It was three weeks ago last Wednesday. Three weeks of peace and quiet."

"Then they only lived here about a month?"

"That was long enough for me to know what kind of man he was. That poor wife of his. Don't think he slapped her around, but he never treated her very nice, either. Thought more of that dog than he did of her. And then there was that other girl."

"What other girl?"

"The one who came to see him while Laurie was at work. Drove a little red car and went too fast. Frank was on second shift, you see, didn't leave for work until two, two-thirty in the afternoon. But Laurie had to be at the beauty shop by eight-thirty in the morning. So Frank had plenty of time for his foolin' around."

Skeeter was finding out a lot about the Hobsons, maybe more than she wanted to know. She said, "Laurie worked in a beauty shop?"

The old woman nodded. "Up in Decatur."

Skeeter asked, "Do you know where the Hobsons went when they moved?"

"Heard they rented a house in Boyd. I'm afraid I don't know the address."

"That's all right. I'll find them." Skeeter stood up. "I surely do appreciate all your help, Mrs. Culbertson."

"How in the world did you ever become a private eye?"

Skeeter realized Ida Lou Culbertson was hungry for company and that was why she was dragging out the conversation. Most of the time, Skeeter would have been glad to oblige, but it was past the middle of the afternoon by now, and she still had to try to locate the Hobsons and then drive back to Fort Worth. She needed to be getting on about her business.

But she could spare a few more minutes, she decided. Without sitting back down, she said, "That's a long story. I used to be a lawyer. My daddy's a lawyer, and he expected all of us kids to follow in his footsteps. I didn't care for it."

"You like the detective business better, do you?"

"Yes, ma'am, I do. At least I can get out and move around a little sometimes. And I get to meet folks like you."

Ida Lou Culbertson smiled. "That's mighty nice of you to say, honey. I hope I was able to help you."

"You surely did." Skeeter stepped down off the porch. "I've got to be going now. Goodbye, Mrs. Culbertson."

"You stop back by any time, you hear?"

"Yes, ma'am, I'll do that."

As Skeeter went to her pickup, she heard Ida Lou Culbertson saying, "A private eye, just like Shell Scott . . . Well, I'll do know!"

Chapter Four

It took only a few minutes to drive back down the state highway to the small town. She planned to return to the post office and find out if Frank Hobson had filed a forwarding address after his last move, but before she reached it, she spotted something down a cross street that made her hit the brakes and swing the pickup into a turn.

A house about halfway down the block was surrounded by a sagging chain-link fence, and on the fence was a large handmade sign that read BEWARE OF DOG. There were smaller letters under those three words, and as Skeeter pulled up in front of the house, she could make them out. *No Trespassing—Not Responsible for Bites or Other Accidents.*

Skeeter turned the engine off and stepped out of the pickup. It was pushing the limits of coincidence to think that she could spot the very place she was looking for just by driving past it, but she had seen enough to know that damn near anything could happen in life, coincidental or not. The mailbox was right beside the front fender of the pickup, and she had to step past it to reach the gate in the fence. The day's mail had already been delivered; she could see it through the half-open mailbox door. Sometime in the past, somebody had played a game of mailbox baseball along here, and it looked like this box had been good for a three-bagger, at least. It had had some of the dents pushed out of it and had been set back on its post, but it would never close properly again.

Pausing just long enough as she went past to peer into the box, Skeeter saw the address label on a magazine. The computer-generated label read *Frank Hobson.*

Skeeter leaned on the fence and looked at the house and yard. The grass inside the fence needed cutting. The house was brick, with a small cement porch by the front door. The paint on the wood trim was starting to curl a little, but it wasn't a bad looking place—if you didn't pay attention to the torn-up plates and chunks of rawhide scattered all over the front yard. What had once been a lawn chair, Skeeter thought, was torn to shreds. And there were other, less fragrant canine souvenirs deposited everywhere she looked.

But no dog.

Skeeter stood there. She could get in the pickup and drive back to Fort Worth, satisfied with what she had found. She could report to Tracy Roberts that evidently Raider was still well out of the county, and Lars Gilford could submit a bill for a day's work on behalf of the agency. Simple as that.

But for some reason, Skeeter wanted to actually see the son of a bitch.

Good choice of words, she told herself as that thought ran through her mind.

Considering all the destruction, Raider was obviously here. But until Skeeter saw him with her own eyes, she was going to have some doubts.

Still leaning on the fence, she called, "Hello? Anybody home?"

There was no response from the house. Skeeter tried again, with the same lack of results. But more importantly, the dog didn't show up, either.

Skeeter frowned. The chain-link fence ran all around the place, from the looks of it, and if Raider was any kind of watchdog, he should have come around from the back whenever she called and announced her presence. He might be penned up in a cage that Skeeter couldn't see from here.

Maybe it would be safe to go in and ring the doorbell. She'd be all right if she just watched where she put her feet, she told herself.

She lifted the latch on the gate, swung it open, and stepped into the yard.

A small bell she hadn't noticed being attached to the gate made a jingling noise as she shut it behind her. Skeeter looked down at it for a moment, then shook her head and started toward the porch on a cracked cement sidewalk.

Raider came around the corner of the house.

For a split-second, Skeeter's mind flashed back to the dogs that had come running at Ida Lou Culbertson's place. She felt the same instinctive surge of fear at the sight of a large, sleek animal coming toward her at a dead run, saliva drooling from its jaws. Raider wasn't grinning like Ida Lou Culbertson's dogs had been, though. And this time the fear was completely justified.

"Ohhhhhhhhhhh, *damn!*"

Skeeter had long since figured out those would probably be her last words on earth, but she hadn't been expecting to utter them this soon. Before they were out of her mouth, she had whirled around and was sprinting for the gate. The dog wasn't barking, and that made the situation even more unnerving. Skeeter couldn't hear the traffic from the nearby highway anymore. All she could hear were her boots thudding against the concrete walk, the breath rasping in her throat, and the soft panting of the dog as it came after her.

Her hand reached out, slapped up the latch. She slammed into it, almost losing her balance as she went through the opening. With an instinctive move, she grabbed the top of the gate and threw it closed behind her. The latch fell.

A fraction of a second later, the fence shivered along its entire front length as Raider crashed against the gate. Skeeter spun around, backing against the bed of the pickup and fumbling for the door handle. The dog rebounded from the impact and threw itself against the fence again. Now the barking and growling started.

The animal was dark brown, with the thick body and massive head common to its breed. Skeeter could well imagine why Tracy Roberts' nephew was still having nightmares. She was plenty upset herself, and there was a fence between her and the dog.

But not a very sturdy-looking fence, Skeeter realized. Maybe it was time to get back in the pickup.

"Are you all right?"

Skeeter heard the voice over the uproar Raider was causing, and she turned her head to see where it had come from. She saw a woman standing in the yard of the house across the street.

Keeping an eye on the dog, Skeeter slid along the pickup and then stepped around to the other side of it. Raider quieted down a little as she moved out of his sight, but he was still barking and snarling. Skeeter walked across the road. She realized that despite the chill in the air, she was sweating.

"Did the dog bite you?" the woman asked as Skeeter walked up to her. "I wish I'd seen you drive up. I would have told you that Frank and Laurie aren't home and that you shouldn't go into the yard."

"Well, I saw the sign with my own two eyes," Skeeter said, summoning up a smile. "Got nobody to blame but myself for nearly getting eat up. You know the people who live there?"

"Of course. Not well, but I always try to get to know all of my neighbors. Were you wanting to talk to the Hobsons?"

Skeeter fell back on the same story. "I've got a delivery for them."

"Do you want to leave the package with me?"

"Thanks for the offer, but it's a C.O.D.," she added so the woman wouldn't offer to sign for the nonexistent package.

"Oh. Well, in that case . . . Do you want me to tell them you came by?"

Skeeter shook her head. "That's not necessary." To keep the conversation going, she said, "That's one of those pit bulls, isn't it?"

"Yes, and it's vicious even for that kind of dog. The whole street is terrified of it. We've had several pets disappear, you know, smaller dogs and cats, and I'm certain that animal's to blame. I wish he'd get rid of it, especially after what happened to Laurie."

Skeeter tried not to show any more than casual interest. "What was that?"

"Raider bit her last week. Took a chunk out of her leg for no reason at all. Frank had to take her down to the hospital in Azle, to the emergency room. They stitched it up and gave her some shots. Frank made her claim she tore her leg open on the kitchen table. He wouldn't let her admit that the dog did it. He said he wasn't going to go through all that quarantine business again when he knew perfectly well there was nothing wrong with Raider. I think he thought the whole thing was sort of, well, funny. Ha-ha funny, you know what I mean?"

Skeeter nodded.

"I think he was proud of what he and the dog had both done, the way he was talking about it to his friends. I had the windows open, and I heard him standing right there in his front yard and telling those men in the fancy car about it. That's how I know about the story he made Laurie tell the doctors. I'm sure they could tell it was a dog bite, but when she insisted otherwise, what else could they do?"

"Well, I know one thing," Skeeter said. "I wouldn't go

back in that yard, not for what they're paying me to deliver packages." She started back toward the pickup. "Guess I'd better be going."

"Nice talking to you," the woman called after her.

Skeeter hadn't really learned anything new except for the business about Raider biting Laurie Hobson. And evidently, the friends who had visited Frank up at the Culbertson mobile home had followed him here to his new place in Boyd. Skeeter was curious about them.

Curious or not, this case was over. When she reached the pickup, a thought occurred to Skeeter as she opened the door. She had a folding Polaroid camera in the glove compartment, a pretty standard piece of equipment for a private detective. She could take a picture of the dog to help document his whereabouts and further ease Tracy Roberts' mind. A glance back across the street told her that the neighbor had gone inside. Skeeter reached over to the glove compartment, opened it, and took out the camera.

Raider stayed where he was as she edged toward the back of the pickup and focused the camera on him over the top of the truck bed. Evidently, once he had calmed down it would take the jingling of the bell on the gate to set him off again. Skeeter had already figured out that Hobson must have trained the animal to attack only when he heard that sound.

She heard a squeal of tires as she snapped a picture of Raider, the camera spitting the photographic paper out the slot in the front to let the air develop it. Skeeter looked to her right and saw a yellow Toyota pickup coming up fast behind her vehicle. The driver braked hard, causing the tires to skid a little in the gravel on the side of the road. Almost before the Toyota had rocked to a stop, the door was thrown open and an angry male voice demanded, "Hey, what the hell do you think you're doing?"

JAMES REASONER and LIVIA J. WASHBURN

Skeeter knew without being told that this was Frank Hobson. He was an inch or so taller than her, with a broad, florid face and curly brown hair. There was several days' worth of graying beard stubble on his cheeks and jaw. He was big but not really fat; his bulk looked to be muscle. Even at a distance of several feet, Skeeter could smell the beer on his breath.

She hefted the camera. "This, you mean?" she asked with a smile. "I was just taking a picture of that dog," she said, stating the obvious. "That's a mighty fine-looking animal."

The compliment eased the anger on Hobson's features. "Think so, do you?"

"I sure do. Is he yours?"

"Damn right."

"Do you think you'd be interested in doing some breeding?"

The anger on Hobson's face disappeared completely. He broke into a grin as his eyes dropped to Skeeter's breasts. He said, "That depends."

"I was talking about the dog."

"Sure you were."

Skeeter glanced at the Toyota, from which a woman was getting out on the passenger side. As Skeeter watched, she slammed the door and went around to the back of the truck to lift a sack of groceries out of the bed. "I'm going to take these inside, Frank," she called.

"Yeah, go ahead," Hobson said without taking his eyes off Skeeter. He asked her, "You got a pit bull bitch?"

She nodded. "My daddy and I are just getting started raising 'em. I was driving by and saw that dog of yours. Thought I'd get a picture of him so I could show Daddy what a proper animal looks like."

"Ol' Raider's a dandy, all right. He can do the job for

you," Hobson said proudly. "Ain't nothin' he likes better. 'Cept maybe fightin'." Hobson hitched up his pants. "He takes after his daddy."

Skeeter wasn't sure if he was referring to the dog's sire or to himself. She glanced at the house. Laurie Hobson had gone through the gate and was now standing on the porch, unlocking the front door. Raider was several feet away from her and seemed to be ignoring her, but Laurie kept shooting nervous glances at the dog. Skeeter didn't blame her.

"Why don't you give me your phone number?" Hobson went on. "I'll call you and we'll set up a time for you to bring that bitch over."

"Good idea. You might give me your number, too."

Hobson shook his head. "We don't have a phone yet. Just moved in a few weeks ago. But don't worry, I'll get in touch with you."

"That'll be fine." Skeeter tossed the camera through the open window of the pickup onto the seat, then took a small spiral notebook from her shirt pocket and tore out a sheet. She made up a name—Linda Mae Shively—and a telephone number, scribbled them on the sheet with her pen, and handed the paper to Hobson.

He glanced at it, grinned again, and said, "I'll give you a call, Linda."

"I'll be waiting." Skeeter lied then opened the door of the pickup.

"Be seein' you," Hobson called as Skeeter got in the truck and started the motor. She lifted a hand in a wave of farewell as she swung the pickup into a U-turn and started toward the highway half a block away. As she passed the Toyota pickup, she saw Laurie Hobson taking another bag of groceries from the back of it.

Skeeter heaved a sigh of relief as she turned onto the

highway. Now the job was really complete.

But as she drove toward Fort Worth, she found herself wondering about a few things. Who were the men in the fancy cars who had visited Hobson first at the trailer house and now at his place in Boyd? What about the girl in the little red car? Had she followed him to Boyd, too? And now, as Skeeter thought about what Tracy Roberts had told her the day before, she asked herself how somebody who worked at Lockheed, somebody who rented rundown places and drove a pickup that was more than ten years old, how that somebody could afford a high-powered lawyer to keep his dog and himself out of trouble? Hobson just hadn't seemed to be the type who could afford high legal fees.

All that was none of her business, she knew. She had done what Tracy Roberts wanted. Her curiosity about everything else didn't have to be satisfied in order to bring the case to a successful conclusion.

Skeeter just wished she didn't feel quite so antsy about the whole thing.

Chapter Five

Lars Gilford had been happy with the results of her trip. The Roberts contract was in the wire-mesh basket marked *Current Cases;* she picked it up and got Tracy Roberts' phone number from it. She might not be home—she'd said she was a secretary, and it wasn't quite five o'clock—but Skeeter thought it was worth a try.

A breathless female voice answered the phone after the third ring. Skeeter asked, "Mrs. Roberts?"

"Yes?"

"This is Cassandra Barlow at the Hallam Agency. I've got good news for you about that dog. The Hobsons are living up in Boyd, so I don't think you or your sister or her little boy have to worry about Raider anymore."

"Thank God," Tracy Roberts said fervently. "I really didn't trust that man. It would've been just like him to move back here into town without telling anyone."

"Well, there's no telling what he'll do in the future, but right now you don't have anything to worry about."

"You've made my day, Ms. Barlow." Tracy Roberts gave a tired little laugh. "There's nothing like some good news after a hard day at work. I'm going to call my sister and see if she and Joey would like to go out and do something fun this weekend."

"Sounds good," Skeeter told her. "You'll be getting a full report in the mail, along with our statement."

"Thank you. I really appreciate everything you've done, Ms. Barlow."

"You're welcome." Skeeter grinned, even though Tracy Roberts couldn't see the expression over the phone. "You ever need any more private eye work done, you come see us, you hear?"

"All right, I'll do that. Goodbye."

Skeeter said goodbye and hung up, then glanced at her watch again. There would be plenty of time to get the official report written up before she left for the day. She switched the computer on, checked the files, and found that Tommy had already made one for the Roberts case. The boy was nothing, if not efficient. Skeeter typed her findings into the file, saved them, then swapped files and started working up the bill for Tracy Roberts. It was simple enough—one day's wages and a little expense money for the trip to Boyd and the single long-distance phone call she'd made. The total came to less than four hundred dollars. Skeeter hoped the client was pleased.

As for her, she had a Friday night at the Horsehead facing her. It was time to put this job behind her and concentrate on the one coming up.

There was already a good crowd in the place when Skeeter came in. Jasper and Chuckie were behind the bar, along with a third bartender named Dave. Several waitresses hurried around the room, delivering drinks to the tables. Jasper nodded to her as Skeeter started a circuit of the room, swaying her hips to the beat of the music.

She sang to herself as she passed one of the tables, but she stopped abruptly as a hand reached up and rested itself on the taut denim over her rear end.

Skeeter looked down at the man. There were three couples sitting at the table. One of the women had an angry expression on her face as her companion fondled Skeeter, but the other four people at the table were laughing drunkenly. The man who was touching her had a silly grin on his face.

"Listen, sport," she said calmly, "I don't recall askin' you to put your hand on my rear. I think I'd remember a lapse of judgment like that."

The comment brought a smile to the face of the woman who had looked mad a moment earlier. Her companion's grin faltered a little, and he asked, "You mean you don't like it?"

"As long as you're holding it still, I reckon I can tolerate it. You go to wigglin' those fingers, mister, and I might have to break a few of 'em."

"Get your hand off her butt, Harry," said the man's date or wife or whatever she was to him. "You've demonstrated how suave and sophisticated you are."

"Hell, Doris, don't start talkin' to me like that," Harry snapped. "You ain't Miss Culture of Tarrant County."

The other two men hooted.

Harry warmed to the encouragement. "When was the last time you was at the opera or the ballet, huh? Tell me that, Doris. Or how about the damn symphony?"

At least arguing with Doris had gotten Harry's mind—and his hand—off Skeeter. She moved on.

There were no more incidents as she made her way around the room and back to the bar. A couple of men asked her to dance, and she turned them down each time with a grin and a joke. Keep it light, keep it fun . . . keep folks from killing each other.

She spotted a couple of familiar faces at the bar and went down the length of the hardwood to its end, catching Jasper's eye along the way. She had only been leaning on the bar for a few seconds when he worked his way down to her. "Problem?" he asked.

"I'm not sure," Skeeter said. "There's cops in here."

"Who are you talking about?"

Skeeter nodded toward the two young men sitting at the bar, about halfway along it. They looked like a lot of the other customers in the Horsehead, fairly clean-cut, wearing new-looking jeans, Western shirts, and hats. Jasper frowned a little as he studied them.

"You sure?" he asked Skeeter.

"I've seen 'em around before, downtown. They work vice. Could be they're off-duty and like country music. Could be they're undercover for some reason."

Jasper's frown deepened. Vice cops were regular visitors to the Horsehead, checking for liquor violations and drug use and dealing, but usually they didn't dress like the club's clientele. Skeeter could tell he was bothered by the situation. Nobody ran a cleaner club than Jasper Lowe, as far as Skeeter was concerned—and she'd seen more than her share of honkytonks over the years—but he still didn't like the idea of cops working undercover in the place.

"Think you can find out if something's up?"

Skeeter nodded. "I'll try."

Before she reached the men she had pointed out to Jasper, they drained the last of the beer from their longnecks, placed the empty bottles on the bar, and stood up. They started toward the door, trying to give the impression of ambling along, but they were moving a little too quickly for that. Skeeter stopped where she was, her eyes narrowing as she watched them leave.

Jasper came along the bar. When he was opposite her, he leaned on the hardwood and said, "What the hell was *that* all about?"

"Damned if I know," Skeeter replied. "I guess they didn't find what they were looking for."

She didn't have time to worry too much about the matter. From one of the tables, a loud voice angrily demanded,

"What the hell's somebody like him doin' in here?"

Skeeter turned around and saw a stocky, bullet-headed man with gray hair leaping up from his chair to confront a taller but much more slender man. She cast a glance toward Jasper, cocked an eyebrow in resignation, and started across the floor to break up the fight that was about to begin.

When she got close enough to hear over the music, the second man was saying, "—didn't mean to cause any trouble. I just wanted—"

"I don't give a damn what you want!" the gray-haired man bellowed. His features brick-red with anger, he went on, "If you don't get out right now, I'm goin' to have to whip you, boy." He was trembling with anger.

Skeeter had almost reached the table. She said, "Whoa! Settle down, fellas. No need for a ruckus."

The men ignored her. The troublemaker demanded hotly, "Are you goin' or not?"

In a quiet voice, the second man replied, "Don't reckon I can do that, friend."

That was the wrong thing to say. Skeeter grimaced as she saw the gray-haired man's face contort in rage. The man's bunched right fist leaped toward the other man's face.

Skeeter lunged forward, hoping to intercept the blow, but before she could get there, another man jumped up from the table and grabbed her around the waist. "Here now, little lady!" he grunted. "You don't want to get mixed up in that!"

Skeeter growled, "Get your hands off me." When she saw he wasn't going to let her go, she kicked back with her right foot, aiming high so she could get the man's shin above the top of his boot. He let out a howl of pain as the heel of her boot smacked sharply into his leg.

By then, Skeeter had hold of one of his thumbs and was twisting it almost to the breaking point. She slid out of his grip and drove an elbow into his jaw. He sagged and went down across the table with a crash.

Somebody yelled, "Fight!" and just like a schoolyard, everybody hurried to watch. As a circle of people formed around the table, Skeeter whirled to see the gray-haired man trading punches with his opponent. The slender man's hat flew off, and Skeeter caught a glimpse of a shock of black hair. As she started toward them again, another of the gray-haired man's companions started to get up, obviously intent on getting in her way. She fixed him with a cold stare and said, "You don't want to do that."

He sank back in his chair.

The gray-haired man connected with a solid right that knocked his opponent backwards and off his feet. Skeeter moved in before the gray-haired man could press his advantage. He stopped short, eyes widening in surprise as he found himself confronted by a large, angry, redheaded woman in a cowboy hat. He muttered, "What the hell—"

Skeeter kicked him in the belly, then as he doubled over, snapped a backhanded blow to the side of his head, just like Bruce Lee in those chop-socky movies she'd watched in countless drive-ins as a teenager. The gray-haired man went down and stayed down.

"What the hell did you do that for?" The furious question came from the third man at the table, the one who had started to interfere and then thought better of it.

"What?" Skeeter snapped, rubbing the knuckles of the hand she had just used. "Bust up a fight some stupid son of a she-wolf started for no reason?"

"Ken had the best reason in the world. He lost two brothers in 'Nam!"

Skeeter frowned.

The man pointed and went on, "You can't blame him for

losin' his temper when he saw that . . . that *gook* in here!"

Skeeter turned. The slender man whose presence had touched off the fracas was picking himself up off the floor. He dusted off his hat, settled it on his head, and wiped away a trickle of blood leaking from his mouth. The Vietnamese features creased in a grin as he said in as pure a Texas twang as Skeeter had ever heard, "Sorry about the ruckus, ma'am. Didn't mean to cause no trouble."

After a couple of seconds, she realized she was staring. Jasper and Chuckie loomed up on either side of her, and Jasper indicated the two men Skeeter had knocked down. Both of them were shaking their heads groggily. "Get 'em out of here, Chuckie," Jasper said. "Their buddy, too."

"That ain't fair," the man still at the table complained. "You're throwin' us out, but you'll let that gook stay?"

"I'm throwin' out three troublemakers," Jasper said in a hard voice. "You need any more explainin' done, mister, you just keep talkin'."

The man looked at Jasper and then at Chuckie, who had gained a little weight since his playing days but still appeared to be quite capable of sacking the quarterback on a max blitz. Swallowing his pride and his nervousness, the man stood up and headed for the door. Chuckie hauled both of the other men to their feet and prodded them toward the exit, too.

Still grinning, the Vietnamese man said to Skeeter, " 'Preciate you givin' me a hand like that, ma'am. I might've been able to handle one of them fellas, but not all three. Can I buy you a drink?"

Jasper answered the question for her. "Skeeter don't drink nothin' but iced tea when she's workin', son, but if you'll come up to the bar, there's a beer waitin' for you—on the house."

"Thanks." The three of them walked back to the bar as the

crowd in the big room scattered out again, going back to their drinking and talking and dancing.

Skeeter and the Vietnamese man took stools in front of the bar while Jasper went behind it and popped the cap on a longneck. He slid it over to the man, then poured a glass of tea for Skeeter. The Vietnamese man lifted the beer and said, "To new friends."

"To new friends," Skeeter echoed. Gratefully, she sipped the tea, then said, "My name's Skeeter Barlow."

"Ngyuen Van Minh. But you can call me Buck." He took a long pull on the beer. "How'd a lady like you learn to fight like that?"

Skeeter shrugged. "A few lessons. A lot of experience."

"Best bouncer in the Southwest," Jasper said, nodding toward Skeeter.

"I've always envied folks who're good at martial arts. People look at me and figure, well, since I'm not from around these parts, let's say, that I ought to be good at things like that." Buck shook his head. "But I never got the hang of it."

Skeeter grinned. "You must have been over here in this country for quite a while."

"Since I was two. I got to grow up a Texan. Learned to speak English from watchin' old Hopalong Cassidy and Roy Rogers movies on TV."

"Good lord," Jasper said. "It's a wonder you don't sound like Gabby Hayes."

"Gabby! My favorite! The sidekick of all sidekicks! Say, do you remember the one where he—"

Skeeter took his hand and pulled him down off the stool as the band took the stage and started getting ready to play. "Come on, Buck," she said. "Let's dance."

Chapter Six

Skeeter stirred, pressed her face deeper into the pillow, and threw out an arm, letting it fall on the other side of the bed. It took her several moments to realize the arm had encountered nothing but sheets. There was nobody beside her.

Was anybody supposed to be there? Skeeter rolled over and moaned. She couldn't remember.

Forcing her mind back to the night before, she recalled sitting around the Horsehead after it closed, drinking with Buck and Jasper and Chuckie. She'd started with beer and moved on to Tequila Sunrises, probably not the wisest course of action, she reflected now. But Buck Ngyuen was just about the funniest man she'd run across in a long time, not to mention being genuinely likeable, and she had enjoyed herself immensely—what she could remember of the evening, that is.

The door of Skeeter's room opened. "Good morning," Rita said brightly. "Or rather, good afternoon."

"Burn in hell," Skeeter muttered from the depths of the pillow. She would have shouted the words except for the fact that loud noises would probably crack her skull.

" 'Jose Cuervo, you are a friend of mine'," Rita sang sarcastically. " 'I like to drink you with a little salt and lime'—"

She broke off and dodged as Skeeter rolled over, launched the pillow at her, and then fell back with a moan. After a moment of lying there with her eyes closed, Skeeter asked, "How'd you know I was awake?"

"I was passing by in the hall a few minutes ago and heard you stirring. Actually, I heard you making noises like you had either a major hangover or a magnificent man in here."

Skeeter sat up sharply, winced and said, "Oh!" When the pain in her head eased and her teeth unclenched, she went on, "Why'd you say that about a man? Did you see anything when I came in last night?"

"Just a falling-down-drunk redhead who woke me up by singing when she came in."

"Then . . . I was by myself?"

"Yeah, if that's what you're worried about. Your virtue is safe, kid."

"I'm ten years older than you," Skeeter growled. "Don't call me kid. And my virtue ain't been safe for nearly as long as you been alive."

"Come on," Rita said, her voice softer and more compassionate now. "I've got a big glass of Diet Dr. Pepper fixed for you. Get some caffeine in your system. Then you'd better eat something."

Skeeter swung her legs out of bed, managed to stand up without falling down, and realized she was wearing her nightshirt emblazoned with a picture of Yosemite Sam, brandishing his six-guns and warning anybody who got too close to back off. She didn't remember putting it on. As she staggered past Rita on her way to the bathroom and then the kitchen, she patted the younger woman on the shoulder and said, "Thanks."

"No problem."

Skeeter glanced at the clock as she went into the kitchen a few minutes later. Nearly one in the afternoon. She yawned. Three aspirin chased down by diet drink. Sit and glare at the tablecloth for fifteen minutes. Some toast, that was what she needed, she decided. Rita left her alone, and by two o'clock, as Skeeter emerged from her bedroom again wearing jeans and a turquoise blouse, she at least felt almost human again.

"So," Rita asked, "what's on the agenda for today?"

"It's Saturday," Skeeter reminded her. "I take it easy and get ready for tonight."

Saturday was the busiest night of the week at the Horsehead—and the most likely time for real trouble to break out.

Actually, the evening went much smoother than Skeeter had anticipated it would. There were no major fights, only a few obnoxious drunks who had to be escorted outside. Other than that, she spent the evening drinking iced tea, munching pretzels, and enjoying the music.

She waited around after the place closed, talking to Jasper until he was ready to lock up and leave. All the other employees were already gone. Skeeter checked the front door, then walked out the back with Jasper. Her pickup was parked next to his old van. As she unlocked the pickup door and stepped up into the vehicle, she waved and called, "See you Tuesday night." The next two evenings were her regular nights off.

Jasper returned the wave, then sat in his van and waited until she had started the pickup and pulled out of the small parking area behind the club. He seemed to be keeping a closer eye on her than usual tonight, she thought as she drove away. Maybe he felt guilty for letting her get so drunk before she started home the night before. But, hell, she was a big girl, and Jasper Lowe wasn't her daddy by any stretch of the imagination.

The streets of downtown Fort Worth were as close to deserted as they ever got. She saw only a few cars moving here and there, an occasional bum shuffling along the sidewalk or sleeping in a doorway. As she passed Throckmorton Street, she saw the flashing lights of a cop car about eight blocks down, parked at the curb. Probably checking out an alarm that had gone off, Skeeter thought.

She wasn't really aware of the headlights behind her until she reached Forest Park Boulevard.

She didn't know how long the car had been behind her. Her foot came down a little heavier on the pickup's accelerator. Skeeter told herself she wasn't really worried. Just because a car had planted itself thirty feet behind her rear bumper and stayed there regardless of how fast or slow she was going, that didn't have to mean anything sinister.

But her foot pressed down harder and harder on the gas pedal anyway.

She swung through the big left-hand curve opposite Trinity Park and came up on an intersection. The light was blinking red at this time of night, rather than going through the usual green-yellow-red sequence. Skeeter ignored it, driving on through the intersection instead of stopping as she legally should have.

She was getting mad now, and she wished she had a gun in the car. The freeway was just ahead. If the people following her were going to make a move before they got there, it would have to be quick.

But the other vehicle stayed where it was, trailing her without coming any closer. The light was red at the freeway. Skeeter ignored it, too, and wheeled the pickup into the sharp turn leading to the entrance ramp. This particular entrance could be a pain during rush hour, but now she was able to get on the freeway with no trouble. She pushed the pickup from seventy to seventy-five, then to eighty. It didn't do any good; the tail stayed with her.

Skeeter decided to quit being mad and start being scared. She put the pedal on the floor and hung on tight to the steering wheel. Green exit signs flashed by.

She saw a police car up ahead, parked on the side of the freeway, and her foot instinctively jerked up off the accelerator. The next second, she stomped it again, sending the pickup shooting forward with only a slight lurch.

She drove by another exit, then passed the cop car going eighty-five. Red and blue lights bloomed in the night, looking a little strange and sickly in the yellow-orange glow from the big sodium vapor lights along the freeway. Skeeter hit the brakes, slowing down gradually and steering toward the shoulder of the road.

In the rearview mirror, beyond the fast-closing cop car, she saw headlights swing off the freeway on the exit she had passed moments earlier. The pursuers had spotted the police, too, and were breaking off the tail job.

Skeeter brought the pickup to a stop and drew a deep, shaky breath. She was parked on the slope of an embankment leading up to an overpass, and as she looked down at the service road to her right, she saw the car pass by. It was a nondescript sedan, eight or ten years old, and there were two men in it.

Both of them were wearing cowboy hats.

Didn't mean a damn thing, she told herself as the police car came to a stop behind her pickup. Didn't mean that the men who had followed her tonight had been the same two vice cops who had been in the Horsehead the night before.

For some reason, she would have been willing to bet that was the case.

She rolled her window down as the two officers got out of their car and approached, the one on the right hanging back with his hand on the butt of his revolver, just like he was supposed to. The one on the left stopped before he got to her window and said, "Sort of late at night to be in such a hurry, ma'am."

Skeeter kept her hands in plain sight on top of the wheel, turned her head, and said, "Did you see those fellas chasing me?"

"As a matter of fact, we did. Did they try to hurt you?"

"Not really. They just got on my tail downtown and weren't getting off."

"I'll need to see your license anyway, ma'am."

Skeeter reached for her purse. She might get out of this without a speeding ticket, since she had been lucky enough to run across some cops who were paying attention to something else besides their radar gun. But even if she had to pay a fine and got her insurance rates jacked up, it might be worth it.

Those two cowboys had had *something* in mind. She just wished she knew what it was.

As it turned out, the cops used common sense and let her go without giving her a ticket or even a warning. They even followed her back to her house to make sure the cowboys didn't show up again and try anything else. Skeeter still felt a little shaky as she locked the pickup, waved at the two cops as they drove slowly by, and went into the house. Everything was quiet, and Rita was sound asleep in her bedroom.

Skeeter took her clothes off, showered quickly, and fell into bed, expecting to drop right off to sleep. She was still too keyed-up, though, and her mind kept asking questions. Were the cowboys the same two vice cops? If so, why had they been following her? The previous night, she had figured that they were in the Horsehead on business, but it hadn't occurred to her that *she* might be the reason they were there.

It didn't make a whole lot of sense.

By the next morning, it still didn't. Skeeter told herself to forget about it. The incident was over, and no harm was done. By evening, she even had herself half-convinced that her pursuers hadn't been the two cops from the Horsehead.

The week rolled on uneventfully for Skeeter. Buck Ngyuen hadn't been in the Horsehead since Friday, and as she went to work Thursday night, Skeeter found herself hoping he would show up. A talk with him might be just what she needed to lighten her mood. She glanced toward the door from time to time, but he didn't come in.

Skeeter felt antsy again. If she'd believed in such things, she might have said that her woman's intuition was kicking up, making her nervous over something that was about to happen. She'd never put much stock in stuff like that, though. Might as well believe in stories like the one about the little spaceman being buried in the Aurora cemetery.

She went to the ladies' room during one of the few lulls when the jukebox was silent. By the time she came out, the music was blasting loudly again. Skeeter skirted the dance floor, stepped up onto the deck in front of the bar, and leaned on the hardwood, motioning to Jasper for another iced tea. He set the glass in front of her and started to say something, but a customer down the way demanded attention. He shrugged and said, "Be right back, Skeeter."

She nodded and sipped the tea. Suddenly, a voice that was vaguely familiar said from behind her, "Skeeter? I thought your name was Linda."

Skeeter looked over her shoulder. Standing there with a confused frown on his face was Frank Hobson.

Chapter Seven

Skeeter's first thought was *How'd he get in here?*, then she realized he must have come into the club while she was in the ladies' room. Her mind went back six days to their only previous meeting, trying to remember the rest of the name she had given him. Shively, that was it, Linda Mae Shively.

She put a big grin on her face and said, "Hey, how you doin'?"

Hobson shrugged. "Not too good." He still looked suspicious. "I asked how come that guy called you Skeeter?"

"Well, that's my name, silly. Or at least that's what people call me. My friends, anyway. You can call me Skeeter."

With a nod, Hobson moved onto the stool next to her, even though he hadn't been invited. Skeeter had a feeling he wasn't the type to wait for very many invitations. At least he seemed satisfied with the explanation she had given him about her name.

Jasper came back down the bar, and as he approached, Skeeter caught his eye and tried to look meaningfully at Frank Hobson. She hoped Jasper would understand that he was supposed to follow her lead.

As Jasper paused in front of him, Hobson grunted, "Bring me a beer."

"What kind?"

Hobson shook his head. "Anything. Coors, I guess."

"You got it." Jasper uncapped the bottle and slid it over. "Run a tab for you?"

"Yeah, I guess you better."

Jasper looked over at Skeeter. "Anything else for you, ma'am?"

She shook her head. He'd give her the business about this later, she figured. With a wry little tilt of his eyebrows, he moved off down the bar.

"Guy a friend of yours?" Hobson asked.

"I'm in here fairly often, so we know each other, but that's all." Hobson was acting like he didn't know she worked here, and she'd like to keep it that way. She went on, "Say, I've been waiting for you to give me a call about that dog of yours."

Hobson's face hardened and he said, "Wouldn't've done you any good. Raider's dead."

"Dead?"

Hobson lifted the beer bottle with a hand that trembled slightly, took a long pull from it, replaced it on the bar. "Yeah. Since last Saturday."

"Was he . . . run over by a car?"

"Nope." Hobson hunched his shoulders and stared down at the bottle in his hand. "Damn," he shuddered. "Somebody cut his throat like he was some sort of . . . animal."

Skeeter bit back the obvious reply. "I'm sorry," she lied.

"I picked up Laurie at work and we came home and there he was on the back porch, blood all around him."

Skeeter didn't know what to say, so she just kept her mouth shut and wore a mask of vague sympathy on her face.

Hobson's hand tightened on the bottle. "I'd like to get hold of whoever did it," he rasped. A shiver ran through him, making his brawny shoulders move up and down for a second. "I been drinkin' a lot since then, tryin' to forget the good times me and that dog had together. It . . . it's like losin' a son."

The man had thought it was funny when Raider took a

hunk out of his wife's leg, but he was all broken up about it when the dog died. Something in that man's head just wasn't right, Skeeter told herself.

"Have a drink with me?" he asked. "I'm supposed to meet some fellas and talk business, but I'm early."

She lifted the tumbler of iced tea. "Thanks, but I've already got one."

"I'll buy you another," he insisted. Motioning to Jasper, he said, "Bartender, bring this little lady another of whatever she's drinkin'."

Jasper glanced at her, and Skeeter gave a minuscule nod of her head. The mood he was in, it might be better to play along with Hobson until he met his friends and left. Jasper poured another iced tea for her.

Some of Hobson's grief for Raider seemed to have disappeared. He leaned closer to her and said quietly, "I been thinkin', Linda. You and me, we're two of a kind. Anybody can tell that by the way we both feel about dogs. After I'm done with those guys I'm supposed to meet, what say the two of us go out on the town?"

She'd have rather been exiled to Dallas or Houston for the rest of her life, but she didn't say that. Instead, she told him, "I'm sorry, Frank, I can't."

"Why the hell not? You worried about me bein' married? Laurie don't care what I do. Come on, Linda. We could have us a good time."

His hand came down on her leg, squeezing just above her knee through the fabric of her jeans. It was all she could do to stay motionless.

"I'm sorry, I just can't," she said, wondering where she was getting the politeness in her voice when what she wanted to do was call him a no-good, two-timing snake. "You see, I'm sort of . . . involved with somebody else."

He shrugged, then shook his head and chuckled. "Well, can't blame me for tryin'."

The heck she couldn't, Skeeter thought.

"I've been so depressed since Raider was killed. Thought maybe you could help cheer me up." He glanced at her out of the corner of his eye, trying to see if the pity approach was doing any good. It wasn't.

Before the situation got any worse, somebody called his name and Hobson swiveled around to look at two men who had just come into the Horsehead. He sighed.

"There's my buddies. Guess I'd better go talk to 'em. You still be here when I get through?"

Skeeter shook her head. "I don't know."

"Well, if you're not, maybe I'll see you again sometime."

Not if she saw him coming first, Skeeter vowed. Hobson slid off the stool and walked down off the deck to meet his friends. The three of them went over to a vacant table and sat down. Skeeter watched them in the mirror behind the bar, not sure why she was interested unless it was just habitual curiosity.

One of the men was tall and slender, with thick black hair under the cowboy hat he thumbed to the back of his head as he sat down. The other was shorter and stockier, a gimme cap perched on his dusty blond hair. The one in the cap wore jeans and a flannel shirt, while the first man sported a fancy, light blue bib-front shirt over his jeans. Neither of them looked particularly happy as Frank Hobson sat down and started talking to them. In fact, they looked downright mad, Skeeter thought. Hobson was talking fast, too, like he was in some sort of trouble with them and trying to slicker his way out of it.

Jasper wandered up on the other side of the bar, leaned his elbows on the hardwood, and said, "Who was that, a new boyfriend? You don't tell folks your right name anymore, Skeeter?"

"Boyfriend?" The word tasted bad in Skeeter's mouth when applied to Frank Hobson. "Not hardly. That's the fella who had that pit bull I was checking on."

"He *had* the dog?"

Skeeter sipped her iced tea. "That's right. Somebody killed it."

"From what little you said about the case, I reckon that's good riddance."

"I'm not so sure. Losing the animal's really got Hobson bent out of shape. That might be more dangerous in the long run than having Raider around."

"Who do you think did it?" Jasper asked.

"Don't know. The way things had been going, I might've thought that Hobson's wife killed the dog, but from the way he was talking, she was with him when it happened."

"Well, it ain't none of our business, long as the ol' boy doesn't cause any trouble in here."

Jasper was right and Skeeter knew it, but her eyes kept straying to the table where Hobson was sitting with the two other men. A waitress had brought beers for all three of them, but it didn't look like Hobson had touched his. He was still too busy trying to convince the other two of something. Finally they started to nod and smile a little bit, and Skeeter thought Hobson's face took on a look of relief, even though she couldn't see his features very well in the mirror. He reached for his beer and took a long swallow of it.

The other two pushed their chairs back and stood up, each of them saying something to Hobson as they did so. Hobson nodded in agreement and waved as they left. He didn't really relax, though, until the door had shut behind them. Then he looked around, spotted Skeeter at the bar, and got to his feet.

She looked down at the bar and grimaced. Hobson was nothing if not persistent, and she wasn't at all surprised when he sat down next to her again.

"Get your business done?" she asked.

"Oh, yeah," Hobson replied casually. "No problem."

That wasn't the way it had looked to Skeeter, but she didn't say anything.

Hobson went on, "I was just thinkin' we still ought to get together, even if Raider is dead. We might be able to do each other some good."

Skeeter took a deep breath and held a tight rein on her temper. "I told you, I'm involved with somebody—"

Hobson cut her off with a wave of his hand. "That's not what I mean. You said you and your daddy were raising pit bulls, and I know some folks who might be interested in buying some of them from you." He took a business card and a pencil from his shirt pocket and scribbled something on the back, then handed the card to her. "Why don't you come up there this Sunday afternoon, 'bout two o'clock? Give the card to the fella at the gate and he'll let you in. You can do a little business, and who knows, you might get a kick out of the action."

Skeeter glanced at the front of the card. All it said was *Rising Star Ranch, Decatur, Texas.*

"Just go east out of Decatur on Highway 380 about five miles," Hobson said. "Gate's on the left. You can't miss it. Think you'll be there?"

"I . . . don't know." Some impulse made Skeeter say abruptly, "I'll try to be."

Hobson grinned. "Hope so. You won't regret it." He stood up and said, "See ya," then started toward the door.

Skeeter turned the card over to the back again and saw that he had written, "This pretty redhead is all right," then signed his name. She frowned. What the devil . . . ?

A glance at the door told her that Hobson was just pushing through the opening, heading for the parking lot. She slid off the stool and hurried after him. She wasn't sure what she had almost gotten mixed up in, but she knew she didn't want any part of it. She was going to give him back the card and tell him, in no uncertain terms, to leave her alone in the future.

Skeeter opened the door, stepped through the little foyer, and went through the outer door into the night. From the outside, the Horsehead was an old brick building with a neon sign and a good-sized parking area in the front. Skeeter spotted Hobson's yellow Toyota pickup among the other cars and trucks. It was parked about halfway between the building and the street, and Hobson had just gotten to it. He was reaching for the door handle.

Headlights flicked on and a car pulled out a few spaces past the Toyota. Hobson turned to glance at it, then shrunk back against his truck as the car rocked to an abrupt halt behind the Toyota.

Just outside the doorway of the club, Skeeter glanced around. Cars were passing by in both directions out on North Main, but nobody else was in the Horsehead's parking lot at the moment. Instinct made Skeeter slide over into the shadow cast by one of the pillars that supported an awning.

Three men got out of the car that had blocked Hobson's pickup. Hobson's head jerked from side to side, like he was looking for a place to run or a place to hide and couldn't find either one. With a note of forced joviality he said, "Hey, Chris. I was hoping I'd run into you."

One of the three men said something—Skeeter couldn't make out the words—and the other two moved toward Hobson.

Hobson had guts, Skeeter had to give him that much. He

didn't wait for the two bruisers to reach him. Instead, he lunged forward, swinging a wild punch at one of them. The man dodged it easily and rammed a fist into Hobson's belly. He followed the punch with a hard right to Hobson's jaw that straightened him up and sent him staggering back against the Toyota. The men moved in, throwing short, efficient punches.

The man in the suit stood by, arms folded, watching quietly.

Skeeter could have let out a yell and maybe scared them off. But if she interfered, she might wind up getting what Hobson was getting—or worse.

Finally, the two men stepped back and let Hobson sag to the asphalt of the parking lot. The man in the suit came up to him as he lay there and ground the heel of his right shoe down on the back of Hobson's outstretched hand. "Remember," the man said in a clear, distinct voice. Then he turned and walked back to the car, followed by his two companions. All three of them got in, the blond man by himself in the rear seat, and the car roared into motion. Skeeter stayed where she was as the headlights swept over the front of the club. She didn't think they saw her, but she couldn't be sure. As the car turned toward the street, she edged out enough to see that it had vanity plates. The letters spelled out LIMEY.

She'd only heard one word clearly from the blond man. Did he have a British accent? Skeeter couldn't be sure, but she thought so.

Hobson tried to push himself up onto hands and knees, failed, flopped back down again. He made it to his hands and knees, reached up to grab the fender of the truck, pulled himself all the way to his feet. Fumbling with the key, he got the door unlocked, opened it, and climbed awkwardly into the Toyota. The door slammed weakly behind him. A moment later, the motor cranked into life and the pickup pulled out of the parking lot, weaving a little.

Skeeter took a deep breath. Obviously, she'd almost gotten mixed up in something pretty serious. Hobson was in deep with somebody, that was certain.

Realizing she still held the card Hobson had given her, Skeeter lifted it and rubbed her fingers over it. The Roberts case was over, had been over for nearly a week. Frank Hobson had come back into her life by chance, that was all. There was nothing stopping her from throwing the card away and going on about her business.

But she found herself slipping the card into the pocket of her shirt.

Chapter Eight

Sunday afternoon found Skeeter on a narrow, paved road with a carved wooden sign that read RISING STAR RANCH arched overhead. To the right of the entrance, about ten feet inside the fence, was a large oak. A piece of black fabric was fastened around its trunk five feet off the ground. Skeeter frowned as she looked at it. Somebody had tied a black ribbon, instead of a yellow one, around the ol' oak tree, she thought. A signal of some sort, maybe, but for what?

A man in sunglasses stood leaning against one of the gateposts. He straightened as Skeeter pulled up. The shades were too dark to let her read his expression.

She rolled down the window of the pickup and gave him a smile. "Howdy," she said brightly. "Reckon I've come to the right place?"

"Depends on what you're looking for, ma'am," he said solemnly, a deep voice coming from his barrel chest.

Skeeter was wearing her concho-studded denim jacket. She slipped the card Hobson had given her from one of the pockets and offered it to the guard. That was obviously what he was. She hadn't been able to see it from the highway, but there was a pump shotgun leaning against the backside of the gatepost.

The man took the card, glanced at the front, then turned it over and read the message on the back. His head lifted slightly as he looked up. Checking the color of her hair, Skeeter knew. That was why Hobson had written that business about her being a pretty redhead. It wasn't a compliment—it was a means of identification.

"I'll keep this, ma'am," the guard told her. "You drive right on through. Just stay on this road until you get to the ranch headquarters."

Skeeter smiled at him again and took her foot off the brake. "Thanks," she called as the pickup rolled past him.

The smile dropped off her face and she drew a deep breath as she drove north away from the highway. The road dipped and climbed through the hills, sometimes circling around some of the slopes. The Rising Star was a pretty place, Skeeter thought. She saw quite a few cattle grazing on the hillsides, and she kept her speed fairly slow for that reason. Cows had been known to wander out onto roads from time to time.

She spotted the house up ahead, perched on the summit of one of the small hills. It was a low, rambling Spanish-style structure with whitewashed walls and a red tile roof. On the side of the main house were several outbuildings, including one wooden barn and a couple of smaller metal ones. There were probably more buildings she couldn't see on the far side of the rise, Skeeter thought. The house by itself was likely worth half a million, not even taking into account the thousands of acres of prime ranching land that surrounded it.

On this side of the house was a windowless smaller building, also showing Spanish influence in its design. A couple of dozen vehicles were parked beside it in a gravel-paved parking area. Skeeter wheeled the pickup into the turn-off and let it coast to a stop next to a Winnebago. In addition to the RV, there were pickups ranging from fancy custom jobs to beat-up old work trucks. The cars were a mixture, some domestic, some foreign, all expensive. Skeeter gave them the once-over as she got out of her pickup and ambled toward the door of the building. It was open, and she heard music and laughter coming from inside.

A man and woman emerged from the door before Skeeter could reach it. She recognized the man immediately: he was the tall, dark-haired cowboy Frank Hobson had been talking to in the Horsehead a couple of nights earlier. Today, he wasn't wearing a hat and his spangled and fringed shirt looked like something out of a Roy Rogers movie, but he was unmistakably the same man. He was walking with his left arm around the woman's waist. She wore tight jeans and a lacy white blouse. Her straight dark hair hung halfway down her back, and her features had the sort of delicate beauty that people usually associated with wealth. Both of them stopped and looked curiously at Skeeter as they noticed her approaching.

"Hi," the man said. "Can we help you?"

She gave them a bright smile. "I'm Linda Mae Shively, but my friends call me Skeeter. Frank Hobson asked me to come up this afternoon. Is he here yet?"

"Oh, yeah, Frank's here." The man extended his hand. "I'm Roy Danby, and this is my wife Martina. Glad to meet you, Skeeter."

She shook hands with both of them. Danby's grip was firm but not overly so, Martina's cool and a little limp. The woman seemed friendly enough as she said, "So you're Frank's guest."

"I suppose so," Skeeter said with a shrug. "He said something about there being some people here he wanted me to meet."

"Plenty of good folks here, all right," Danby said enthusiastically. "Welcome to the Rising Star, and you have a good time, you hear?"

"I sure will." They started to move past her, but Skeeter stopped them by asking, "Is this your place?"

"Sure is," Danby replied with a proud laugh.

"We were just on our way up to the house to get some more champagne," Martina added. "You go on in and mingle, Skeeter. We'll be back in a little bit."

Skeeter lifted her hand in a wave as they moved on toward the corner of the building. A paved walkway led from there up the hill to the main house. Skeeter headed toward the door, and as she got closer, she heard another sound coming from inside, an undercurrent she couldn't identify as it blended with the music and talk and laughter. When she reached the door, she paused to look around before going inside.

The place was one big, dirt-floored room. In the center was a large, circular enclosure of some sort, bordered by a four-foot-tall stone wall. People stood around in large and small groups, mingling and drinking like this was some sort of society cocktail party. Most of the guests were wearing Western garb like the Danbys, the outfits obviously expensive and never worn for work. All the women were stylishly coiffed, and jewelry sparkled on their hands and throats in the glow from the overhead lights.

Not everybody in the room looked rich, though. Several men in work clothes stood along the far wall, next to a row of large metal cages with solid partitions between each holding area. That was so the dogs inside the cages couldn't see each other and go completely crazy, Skeeter thought. The animals could still smell each other, however, and that was enough to make them set up a chorus of angry snarls and growls. That was the strange sound she had heard as she came in, she decided.

She couldn't see all the dogs, but the ones she caught glimpses of through the ebb and flow of the crowd all bore a distinct resemblance to Raider. She would have been willing to bet they were all pit bulls. She edged her way into the excited crowd and searched the far wall for Frank Hobson. Sure enough, there he was, standing in front of one of the cages and talking to a man Skeeter recognized as Hobson's second visitor from the Horsehead, the blond man who had been with Roy Danby. Hobson had several colorful bruises on his face from the beating. Skeeter started winding her way toward him.

He saw her coming and grinned. "Hey, you made it!" he said as she stepped up to him.

"Looks like you almost didn't," Skeeter said, nodding toward his bruises. "What happened to you, Frank?"

"Aw, nothin' important. Just a little run-in with some fellas." Hobson chuckled. "You oughtta see the other guys."

Yeah, sure, Skeeter thought. He didn't know that she *had* seen the other guys.

"Well, I'm sorry anyway," she said, trying to sound sympathetic.

"Don't worry about it."

Hobson's companion nudged him in the ribs with an elbow. "You goin' to introduce me to this pretty lady, Frank?" he demanded.

"Sure, sure. Skeeter, this is my buddy Bobby Mack Wade. Bobby Mack, Skeeter Shively."

Bobby Mack Wade whipped off his gimme cap. "Pleased to meet you, ma'am," he said solemnly. His gallantry might have been a little more convincing, Skeeter decided, if his eyes hadn't been all over her breasts.

"How you doin', Bobby Mack," she said, making it a greeting instead of a question.

He answered it anyway. "Better, now that you're here." The 'possum grin on his face was easily the equal of Hobson's. "You ready for some excitement?"

"I can always use some excitement," Skeeter replied.

"You'll see some today," Hobson assured her. "We got some of the best dogs in the state." His expression became more serious, almost pensive. "I just wish Raider was here. He was the best damn fightin' dog there ever was."

Bobby Mack Wade looked solemn, too, and for a second Skeeter thought he was going to hold his cap over his heart and bow his head in memory of Raider's passing. Instead, he clapped the cap back on his head and said, "Raider was a good'un, all right. But we got to move on, Frank. There's other dogs."

"Damn it, there'll never be another Raider." Hobson was getting more worked up. "If I ever get my hands on the son of a—"

Bobby Mack Wade took Hobson's arm, gripping it firmly and saying to Skeeter, "Excuse us, ma'am, but I reckon ol' Frank here could use a drink. We'll see you later, 'fore the action starts."

"I'll be here," Skeeter promised him. She stood and watched as Wade steered Hobson toward a wet bar in the corner of the room.

Skeeter took a deep breath and then glanced down at the dog in the cage in front of which Hobson and Wade had been standing. It was even uglier than Raider, she decided, and its lips were constantly curled in a teeth-baring snarl. Skeeter repressed a little shudder that threatened to run through her and then moved a few steps away. She was supposed to like these animals, she reminded herself.

She could use a drink herself, Skeeter decided. She looked over at the bar and saw that Hobson and Wade had moved a few steps away from it. Each man held a longneck in his hand. A cold beer might get rid of the bad taste growing in her mouth, Skeeter thought. She walked over to the bar, had to wait a moment while a denim-jacketed bartender mixed drinks for a middle-aged couple in front of her, then asked for a longneck of her own. The bartender smiled, popped the cap off one, and handed it to her. She took a long, grateful swallow.

"Well, look who's here," a voice said behind her. She glanced over her shoulder and nearly choked on the beer when she saw the two familiar faces.

The cops from the Horsehead, the ones she was convinced had chased her on the freeway.

They were both smiling, but the one who had spoken went on in a soft voice, "Just keep your mouth shut, Barlow, and there doesn't have to be any trouble."

Skeeter's fingers tightened on the beer bottle, and she felt an urge to bust it over the cop's head. Instead, she said, "You boys got me mixed up with somebody else. My name's Linda Mae Shively."

"Bull," the other one said, just as quietly as his partner. "You're Cassandra Barlow, and we know what you do for a living when you're not at that honkytonk. So let's help each other out, okay? You don't holler wolf and neither will we."

Skeeter studied them for a long moment. They were a lot alike—young, lean, and intense. Both of them were smiling and trying to look pleasant, but she could see something dangerous glittering in their eyes.

Her chin jerked in a slight nod. "Sure, I'll play along. But you and me have got to talk later, fellas. I want to know what's going on."

"You're a smart girl," the one with the mustache said. "You figure it out." The two of them stepped past her to the bar and asked for drinks.

Skeeter moved away from them, looking for a corner where she could catch her breath and get her wits back about her again. Instead Frank Hobson and Bobby Mack Wade loomed up in front of her. Hobson glared over her shoulder and asked, "Were those two guys botherin' you?"

"Who?" Skeeter said innocently. She glanced back at the cops, who were pointedly ignoring her now. "Oh, you mean them? No, they weren't bothering me, just making a little conversation. You know them?"

Hobson frowned a little. "They look familiar for some reason, but I can't place 'em. Reckon Roy and Martina probably invited them."

Skeeter seriously doubted that, but she couldn't say so without making Hobson suspicious. She shrugged.

"Things'll get started as soon as Roy gets back," Hobson went on. "Be sure and get up close so you can see good."

"I'll do that," Skeeter promised.

"Come on, Bobby Mack. Let's check on them dogs." Hobson turned back to Skeeter for one final word. "After the fights, I'll introduce you to those people I was talkin' about who might be in the market for some dogs."

"Thanks." She smiled as the two men went toward the caged dogs.

There was nothing stopping her from getting out of here right now. She had suspected that Hobson was involved in dog fighting, but she had wanted proof she could turn over to the authorities. Evidently, the authorities already knew about what was going on, judging by the presence of the two vice cops from Fort Worth. Thoughts clicked together in her brain. The two undercover detectives were probably on loan from the FWPD to the Wise County Sheriff's Department or the Texas Rangers, whichever agency was coordinating the investigation into the dogfights. The bouts themselves were not only illegal, but there was undoubtedly a great deal of gambling going on, too.

The cops had gotten on Frank Hobson's trail somehow,

and *that* was why they had been interested in her. They had been trying to find out her connection with Hobson and the dogfights. Obviously, sometime after the incident on the freeway, they had discovered she was a private investigator.

So the best thing for her to do, she decided, would be to go ahead and slip out of here, get in the pickup, and put the Rising Star Ranch behind her. If she hung around, she'd just be getting in the way of the investigation.

She took a sip of beer and started sidling toward the door.

Just as she got there, two figures appeared, silhouetted against the bright sunshine outside. Roy Danby said, "Skeeter! You're not leaving, are you?" Martina was beside him. Each of them was carrying a couple of bottles of champagne.

Skeeter started to make some excuse, but Roy tucked one of his bottles under his arm and took her arm with the hand that freed up. "Come on," he said. "As a newcomer, we want to make sure you have a good time."

He was hustling her back toward the center of the room, and Skeeter knew she couldn't pull away without making a scene and drawing attention to herself. She didn't want that, so she let Danby steer her along. He guided her to the stone wall that surrounded the fighting pit.

"This'll be a good place for you to watch," he said. "Just stay right here. We'll be getting started soon."

As he moved off toward the bar with the champagne, Martina paused just for a moment and smiled at Skeeter. "You'll get used to it," she said in a quiet voice.

Was her uneasiness that obvious, Skeeter wondered? She summoned up a smile and nodded.

Taking her first good look at the pit, she saw that the floor of it was a good four feet below the level of the ground, making it eight feet from the top of the wall to the base of the pit. There was a sturdy gate on the far side of the wall, opening onto a short ramp that led down to the dirt floor. The pit itself was some twenty feet in diameter.

Skeeter found herself wondering if any of those dogs could jump eight feet high. Not very likely, she decided. Still, she would have felt a little safer if there had been some sort of fence around the pit that was even higher.

The spectators probably wanted to be as close to the blood and death as possible.

That thought made her jaw tighten. Most of these people *looked* respectable, instead of like the sick bastards they really were.

Roy Danby came back to the pit from the bar and climbed agilely onto the wall. In a loud voice, he called, "All right, folks, gather 'round! I think we're about ready to get started. Everybody got drinks?" A chorus of assent came from the crowd. Danby grinned. "Good. Now get ready to watch some of the best fightin' dogs you'll ever see."

Carrying their drinks, the people arranged themselves around the edge of the pit. Their conversation was quick with excitement. Skeeter glanced toward the back wall and saw Frank Hobson, Bobby Mack Wade, and several other men getting ready to take a couple of dogs out of the cages. They were using long poles with loops of chain on the end of them to get a good grip on the dogs before the doors of the cages were completely opened. Hobson eased one of the dogs out, snapped a thick leash on its studded collar, then led the animal toward the pit. The spectators all stayed well back as one of the workers—dog wranglers, Skeeter supposed they should be called—opened the gate to the pit. Hobson led the dog down the ramp and over to one side, next to the wall. Another man stood outside the pit and held the pole that was attached to the dog. Hobson unfastened the leash and hurried back up the ramp. The man with the pole held the dog where it was. It didn't strain against the chain, but it was still snarling and trembling with the need to attack something.

The same procedure was used to get the second dog down into the pit. When the animals saw each other, their agitation increased, but they didn't try to break away and start the fight prematurely. The second handler scurried out of the pit. The gate was closed and securely latched behind him.

The place had gotten quiet. Everybody was waiting with anticipation for the fight to begin. Skeeter wished she was almost anywhere else but here. The feeling grew as she glanced across at the other side of the pit and saw the two cops standing there, dividing their attention between her and the dogs.

From his position on the wall, Roy Danby said in a hushed voice, "To my left is Beautiful Dreamer, owned by Judy Ferguson of Denton, and to my right is Asa, owned by Roscoe Garner of Fort Worth. Everybody ready?" Danby paused, but no one spoke up. He nodded and went on, "All right, boys . . . *Turn 'em loose!*"

His voice went up to a yell on the last words. The men holding the poles let off the slack on the chains and with practiced twists of the wrist flipped the restraints off the dogs. The animals lunged ferociously at each other, coming together with a crash in the center of the pit.

Skeeter winced at the violence of the collision, but that was only the start. Teeth flashed as they rolled over and over in the dirt, trying for some sort of advantage. Shouts of encouragement echoed from the ceiling of the big, cavernous room. The spectators pressed forward, leaning over the wall for a better view. Skeeter found herself jammed up against the stone barrier, and she had to lean forward to relieve some of the crowding.

Both dogs were quickly bleeding from minor wounds, but blood suddenly spurted as one of the animals locked his teeth in the other's ear and ripped half of it off. The injured dog didn't cry out or flinch, just fought back that much harder.

Skeeter looked around the wall. Everyone looked caught up in the gory spectacle—including the two cops from Fort Worth, she noticed. They were leaning over the wall, too, and rooting as lustily as anybody else. Maybe that was just part of their cover, Skeeter thought wryly, but she wouldn't have bet on it.

Finally, one of the dogs made a fatal mistake and allowed its opponent to get it down. A flashing bite, and more blood spurted, this time from the stricken dog's throat. An eerie sound, part dismay, part triumph, part . . . satisfaction? . . . went up from the crowd. The winning dog kept savaging the body of the loser until one of the handlers got a chain on it and dragged it away with the pole. On the other side of the pit, Skeeter saw a woman quietly weeping into the hands that covered her face.

How could she be so broken up about the outcome? Skeeter asked herself. Surely she had known that if she kept letting her dog be led into that pit, it would die sooner or later.

Money changed hands all around the ring as bets were paid off. There was some grumbling, but most of the crowd seemed pleased with the outcome. Even those who had lost had enjoyed the show.

And it was just beginning, Skeeter realized with a sick feeling in the pit of her stomach as she glanced at the row of cages along the rear wall.

Chapter Nine

Somehow, Skeeter made it through the long afternoon. There were ten fights in all, and she had to stay until they were over. She hadn't been able to see at first, but the door into the building had been closed and locked as the bloody battles got underway. A little extra security to keep anybody from wandering in unannounced, she thought. But at least she was able to get away from the stone wall and stay on the fringes of the crowd after two or three bouts. She sipped beer, watched the spectators, and wondered what sort of people it took to get such avid enjoyment out of brutality and death.

When the competition was over . . . when five dogs had been killed and five more had been badly hurt . . . Roy Danby climbed on the wall again and said, "Thanks for coming today, folks, and we hope you've all had a fine time. And it's not over! If you'll just mosey on outside, you'll find we've got some tables set up for supper. There's barbecue and all the trimmin's, and we'll have a band playing later if anybody wants to dance. Y'all enjoy!"

A round of applause swept the room. Skeeter joined in halfheartedly, still trying to look as enthusiastic as possible but finding it more and more difficult. The thought of sitting down to a barbecue dinner after what she had just witnessed turned her stomach even more. All she wanted was to get out of here.

The door was thrown open again and people began to move toward it. Skeeter joined the crowd, hoping she could get away without being stopped by anyone she knew.

No such luck. A hand gripped her arm. She looked over at Bobby Mack Wade. He said, "Howdy. Frank told me to find you, ma'am, and tell you he'll see you in just a bit. Got to do a little business with the boss first. You just go ahead and enjoy the supper."

Skeeter assumed he was referring to Roy Danby as the boss. When she had seen Danby and Wade together in the Horsehead, they hadn't struck her as employer and employee. Could be Hobson and Wade didn't work for Danby on a regular basis, just as dog handlers during these blood-thirsty tournaments. She made herself smile at Wade and say, "Thanks for letting me know."

Wade was letting his gaze wander over her body again. He said, "Listen, you get tired of ol' Frank, you just let me know. He's been married so long he's startin' to settle down a little. Me, I'm still wild and single."

"I'll remember that," Skeeter told him, wishing he would let go of her. If he didn't get his hand off her arm pretty soon, she was going to remove it any way she had to.

Luckily for both of them, he let go of her and used that hand to tug at the bill of his cap. "See you later, Skeeter." He headed toward the back of the building.

Skeeter sighed in relief and got out the door before any-body else could stop her. Under the big oak trees to the left of the building were several tables loaded down with platters of food. The guests were lined up, helping themselves to the spread and then moving on to take seats at other tables further on. The same sort of music that had been piped into the building earlier was now coming from speakers in the trees. Skeeter dearly loved a good country-and-western song, but not even Hank Williams Sr. coming back from the grave could have made her stay in that place any longer. She turned her back on the tables of food and headed for the parking area.

Nobody bothered her as she unlocked her pickup and got in. She started the engine, looked behind her, and backed up. As she braked and reached for the gear shift lever, still looking through the rear window, she saw Frank Hobson and Roy Danby emerge from the building. She grimaced as Hobson glanced in her direction and called out to her. Better to ignore him, she thought as she shifted into first and moved her foot from the brake to the gas.

Hobson started trotting after her.

Damn it, Skeeter thought as she accelerated, couldn't the boy take a hint? She glanced at the big side mirror and caught another glimpse of him, his face angry now. Suddenly, somebody reached from the milling crowd and took hold of his arm, stopping him and talking urgently to him. Skeeter could barely see who it was.

But she could see enough to know it was one of the vice cops from Fort Worth.

She slammed the base of her right hand against the wheel in anger, steering with the left as she picked up speed away from the ranch headquarters. Surely that cop wasn't telling Hobson that the woman he was running after was really a private investigator. What good would that do him?

Unless what he had in mind was getting on Hobson's good side and finding out even more about the illegal dog fights and the gambling. Skeeter uttered a heartfelt obscenity as that thought crossed her mind. She'd be willing to bet that was exactly what was going on. And she had played right into the hands of the two cops. This whole business had gotten shot to hell, just because she had been curious.

She still didn't know who "Limey" was or why the man had had Hobson beaten up. She didn't care anymore, either. It was none of her affair, and the smartest thing to do would be to put it all behind her—assuming she got off the Rising

Star Ranch all right, that is. If that guard was still on the gate, he probably had a walky-talky stashed somewhere nearby. Danby could call out there and alert him, order him not to let her go through.

This could get serious, Skeeter thought.

But when she came within sight of the gate, there was no guard around. She looked on both sides of the road. Nothing to be seen but an open gate in front of her.

She drove through it cautiously, still halfway expecting something to happen. Nothing did, though, and her foot came down heavily on the gas as she straightened the wheels from the turn onto the highway. By the time she was a quarter of a mile away, she was going eighty, putting as much distance as she could between her and the Rising Star Ranch and the memories of what she had seen there this afternoon.

The shrill ringing of the telephone dragged her out of bed the next morning. For once, Skeeter was almost glad of the excuse to wake up. Her sleep had been restless all night, haunted by dreams of dogs and death. She was on her stomach as the sound of the phone's summons finally penetrated. It was cut off in mid-ring. Skeeter shook her head groggily. Rita must have answered the call.

She moaned as the door of her room opened and Rita said, "Sorry to bother you, Skeeter. Phone call for you."

Skeeter rolled over, worked her feet out onto the floor, and stood up. A glance at the bedside clock told her it wasn't even nine o'clock. "Who the hell's calling in the middle of the night?" she muttered.

Rita was rubbing sleep from her eyes, a little groggy herself. "It's your boss," she said. "And he doesn't sound happy."

"Jasper? Jasper hasn't seen the morning sun for years!"

"Not Jasper. The other one. Mr. Gilford."

Skeeter straightened, blinked, forced her brain to work. Lars Gilford wouldn't call her like this unless there was a serious problem at the agency, a problem involving her, more than likely. She stalked out of the room, went down the hall to the kitchen, and picked up the receiver that Rita had placed on the table. "What's wrong, Lars?" she asked.

"The office was burglarized last night," Gilford replied without preamble. "You'd better get down here right away."

"You called the cops?"

"Not yet." Gilford answered impatiently. "Are you coming?"

She pinched the bridge of her nose and rolled her shoulders, wishing she could make the weary heaviness go away. "I'll be there," she said. "Give me half an hour."

"Make it fifteen minutes." Gilford's voice was almost its usual expressionless self, but Skeeter could hear a slight trembling in his tone. He wasn't the type to be shaken up by a mere burglary. He was *mad*.

Skeeter said again, "I'll be there," and hung up.

She didn't make it in fifteen like he had requested, but it was pretty close.

When she stepped out of the elevator on the third floor, she found Lars Gilford standing there, his arms crossed, bushy eyebrows drawn down in a frown. Obviously, he was waiting for her, and Skeeter wondered fleetingly if he had been lurking out here in the hall ever since he had talked to her on the phone.

"Come on," he said, turning and striding down the hall toward the agency's entrance door. He went into the office, Skeeter following on his heels.

She stopped short. The place was a mess. Chairs were overturned, everything that had been on the reception desk had been swept off onto the floor, pictures were torn down off the walls and thrown onto the floor, their glass shattered and their frames bent.

"Your office is the same way," Gilford said as she stared at the havoc. "The intruder stopped before he got to mine, for some reason."

"Maybe something scared him off," Skeeter suggested.

"Or perhaps he simply found what he was looking for and quit venting his rage."

Hobson. The name leaped into Skeeter's mind. This sort of wanton destruction was just the kind of thing a man like Frank Hobson would do.

She moved on to the office she shared with Tommy Fuller, gasping as she saw what had been done to the computer. The keyboard was smashed to pieces, and the monitor was lying on the floor with a gaping hole in its screen, as if somebody had tried to punt it like a football. All the drawers in the desk had been pulled out, turned upside down, and emptied. The same was true of the file cabinet in the corner. Tommy squatted in the middle of the mess, looking forlorn as he tried to sort it out and occasionally casting a mournful glance toward the remains of the computer. He forced a weak smile onto his face as he looked up at Skeeter and said, "Pretty bad, isn't it?"

Skeeter agreed. She stepped over some debris, moving further into the room, and looked again at the file cabinet. The bottom drawer, T–Z, was still in place. Skeeter frowned as she knelt beside a pile of file folders that had been scattered on the floor. She started pawing through them.

"I hope you have a good reason for adding to the mess," Lars Gilford said from the doorway.

"I think I do. Tommy, you'd already put up the Roberts file, hadn't you?"

"That business about the dog? I'm sure I filed the report; that was over a week ago."

"That's what I figured," Skeeter said. "Best I can tell, it's not here."

Gilford asked, "You're saying that someone broke in here and did all this just to steal one file?"

"I'm saying he came here looking for the file and made this mess just out of sheer meanness."

"He?"

"Frank Hobson."

"The man who owned the dog?"

Skeeter nodded.

Gilford tugged on one eyebrow as he frowned in thought. "Why would he do something like that?"

Skeeter was still putting the line of reasoning together in her head as she said slowly, "He might've found out that I'm a P.I. The file would tell him who hired us to find him. You see, Raider's dead. Somebody killed him."

"Surely Hobson wouldn't think that we . . ."

Skeeter shook her head. "No, probably not. But he could've figured that whoever hired us is the one who killed the dog."

Gilford's frown deepened. "I didn't have any dealings with that Roberts woman myself. Do you think she could have done it?"

"Killed Raider?" Skeeter stood up and shook her head emphatically. "No way. She's not the type. Besides, I don't reckon Raider would've let anybody near enough to cut his throat unless the person was somebody he knew."

Tommy shuddered. "Somebody cut the dog's throat?"

"That's right."

Something else was bothering Gilford. "How would Hobson find out that you're a detective?"

Skeeter hadn't told them anything about running into Hobson at the Horsehead, or about the two vice cops who had tailed her, for that matter. And she hadn't said anything about planning to go to the dogfight up close to Decatur, either. The whole thing would take too long to explain now. "Because I did something stupid," she said without going into detail. "And I'm going to be the one to put it right."

"Well, I'm going to call the police now," Gilford said. "I just wanted to find out if you knew anything about this. Obviously, you do. I'll want you to give the officers a statement about why you suspect Hobson."

Skeeter nodded. She wanted to be out doing something, tracking down Hobson and settling the score with him for what he had done. But it would be better, she decided with a sigh, to stick around and handle things properly.

Gilford went into his office to call the police, and Skeeter pitched in to help Tommy straighten up the mess. They were both kneeling in the center of the floor, trying to put handfuls of files back in some semblance of order, when the muted bell in the reception room rang. "I'll see who it is," Skeeter said.

She stepped to the door of the office and saw Tracy Roberts standing in front of the reception desk, staring around at the destruction. The woman looked pale and somewhat drawn, as if she'd had a bad night's sleep. She jerked her head up as Skeeter stepped into the reception room.

"Mrs. Roberts!" Skeeter exclaimed. "What are you doing here? Is something wrong?" Normally, Skeeter knew, Tracy Roberts would have been at work now.

"Something is very wrong," the woman said, her fingers closing more tightly on the purse in her hands. "Frank Hobson called me late last night. He called several times, in fact. He said—" Tracy Roberts' voice broke slightly. "He said he was going to get even with me for what I did to Raider."

Skeeter grimaced. As soon as she had seen that the Roberts file was missing, she had been afraid that Hobson would start harassing Tracy Roberts. That was the way the man's mind would work. He wouldn't see how ridiculous it was to think that Tracy Roberts could have killed Raider.

"I'm sorry, Mrs. Roberts," Skeeter began. "Everything just got out of hand—"

"I thought it was all over," Tracy Roberts said. "You sent me your report, I sent you a check. That should have been all there was to it."

She was right, Skeeter thought. If she'd only stayed away from Hobson and not let herself get pulled into this other business about the dogfights . . .

Tracy Roberts squared her shoulders. "What are you going to do about it?" she demanded.

Skeeter waved a hand at the destruction in the room. "Hobson's been here," she said. "You can see that for yourself. We've already called the police. When they get here, you can tell them that he's been threatening you."

"He called every hour last night. I didn't get any sleep."

"I'm sorry," Skeeter said again. "If there's anything I can do—"

"There is. Find out who killed that dog."

Skeeter frowned in thought. What Tracy Roberts had just said made sense. Hobson was in a frenzy of rage because he thought Tracy and, indirectly, Skeeter herself had been responsible for Raider's death. If the real culprit could be located, that might defuse some of Hobson's anger.

"That's a good idea," she said. "You could hire us—"

Tracy Roberts interrupted again. "After what happened last time? I'm not sure I can afford to hire you again, Ms. Barlow."

Skeeter heard the anger in the woman's voice, and she

JAMES REASONER and LIVIA J. WASHBURN

wasn't sure she blamed her. She said quickly, "That's not what I meant. You can pay us a dollar as a retainer, just to make things official. That's all."

"Well, in that case . . ." Tracy Roberts was still upset, but Skeeter's offer mollified her a little. "I suppose that would be all right."

"We'll draw up another contract—" Skeeter glanced around at the wreckage of the office. "—if we can find a blank one, that is. I'll pay a visit to Mr. Hobson this afternoon."

"Do you . . . do you think he's really dangerous?"

Skeeter looked around at what Hobson had done in the office and thought about the man calling Tracy Roberts and threatening her all night long. She shrugged and didn't voice the thought that was running through her mind.

Frank Hobson was a lunatic.

Chapter Ten

The police showed up a few minutes after Tracy Roberts left to go to her sister's house. She was too shaken up to return to her home or go to work. It had taken the cops forty-five minutes to respond to Lars Gilford's call. That wasn't bad, considering how the force was understaffed. Gilford and Skeeter both told the same story about how they suspected Frank Hobson. Without going into details, they made it clear that Hobson was involved in one of the cases the agency was working on and that he might be seeking revenge on them.

The cops agreed that Hobson sounded like the most likely suspect. They promised that an order would be issued to pick him up—if he could be found.

Skeeter knew that was a big if.

When the police had gone, Skeeter went into Gilford's office, glad to get away from the mess for a few minutes. As usual, everything was immaculate in here, every item in its place to the millimeter. She sat down in the client's chair and said, "Tracy Roberts has hired us again."

Gilford nodded. "I heard you talking to the woman. Don't you think you should have asked me first before agreeing to represent her interests again?"

"Sorry," Skeeter said with a shrug. "But I can't let Hobson get away with this. Going after him will be easier if we have some official status."

Gilford inclined his head in acknowledgment. He said, "So. Now what?"

"Now I find out who killed that damn dog, and when I do,

I try to get word to Hobson—assuming he's still running around loose."

"I doubt that tracking him down will be very high on the list of priorities for the various law enforcement agencies. After all, his only real crimes so far are breaking and entering, and vandalizing an office."

"Don't forget gambling and helping to organize illegal dogfights. I reckon they'd call that conspiracy."

Gilford raised an eyebrow. "How could I forget those things? I didn't even know them until just now."

"Well, hold on, and I'll tell you all about it."

For the next fifteen minutes, that's what she did, starting with the first appearance of the vice cops in the Horsehead, proceeding on to the freeway incident, Hobson showing up at the Horsehead and getting beaten up on the club's parking lot, all the way through the dogfights on the Rising Star Ranch the day before. Gilford listened to the story with the usual expressionless mask on his face. When Skeeter was finished, he leaned back and steepled his fingers in front of his face. He said, "It would seem to me that things have gotten out of hand."

Skeeter swallowed her irritation. Course things were out of hand. Hadn't he been listening?

"What do you propose?" Gilford asked.

"I told you, I'm going to find out who killed Raider."

"That means discovering who the rest of Hobson's enemies are. You're sure the wife didn't do it?"

"I'm not sure of anything except that Hobson's a crazy son of a she-wolf," Skeeter said, ignoring Gilford's slight frown at her choice of language. "From what he said, though, Laurie was with him when it happened."

"All right. What about the other people where he lives?"

"Everybody in the neighborhood is scared of that dog, at

least according to the woman who lives across the street. I guess one of them could've gotten brave enough to go around back of Hobson's house with a knife. But I wouldn't want to bet on it."

"Then, as *I* said, you're going to have to find out who the rest of the man's enemies are. I've been thinking about that man who had Hobson beaten. You said the license plate on his car read LIMEY? I'd start by checking them out."

Skeeter stood up. "That's what I intend to do. Whoever that fella was, he had a grudge against Hobson, that's for sure. He might've killed Raider . . . or had the dog killed. He didn't strike me as the type to do his own dirty work."

Gilford gestured at his desk. "Why don't you use my phone? I'm sure Tommy is still straightening things up in the other office."

Skeeter perched on one corner of the desk—probably the first time anybody had ever done that in Gilford's office, she thought—and called the Fort Worth office of the Texas Department of Public Safety. Getting someone's name and address when you had their license number was a fairly simple matter if you had the time to go down to the DPS office, fill out a few forms, and pay a fee. It was even simpler when you knew a clerk who worked there and that clerk owed you a favor because you'd gotten her backstage one night after a concert to meet George Strait.

"Hey, Donna, how you doin'? . . . Oh, I'm gettin' by. Think you could run a plate for me? . . . It's LIMEY, L-I-M-E-Y. . . . Thanks."

Skeeter waited for a few minutes, then wrote down the information her friend gave her. She said, "Thanks a bunch, hon. What's that? No, I haven't heard when George Strait's playing around here again. I'll let you know if I do . . . So long." Turning to Gilford, she went on, "That car belongs to

somebody named Crispin Loomis. Lives in north Dallas."
She read off the address in an exclusive neighborhood.

"Loomis, Loomis . . ." Gilford mused. "There's something familiar about that name. Why don't you go see if Tommy could use a hand while I call someone I know on the Dallas force?"

Skeeter nodded and went next door to the other office. Gilford was no ball of fire, but he was a decent P.I. She was confident he'd turn up something on this Crispin Loomis.

To her surprise, Tommy had most of the chaos cleaned up. The file drawers were back in place, and so were the drawers in the desk. The top of the desk was still littered with broken circuit boards and microchips. Tommy hadn't set the wastebasket back upright, either. He was sitting at the desk, staring at the pile of junk that had been a twenty-five hundred dollar computer.

"I'll bet I could fix this thing," he murmured.

"If it was me, I'm afraid I'd fix it with a broom and that wastebasket," Skeeter said.

"You're probably right." His face fell. "It's hopeless."

"Now, I didn't say that. It'd be hopeless for me. Doesn't mean it is for you."

"I'm sure Mr. Gilford will want to just buy a new one."

"I reckon you're right. Which means maybe you could take what's left of that one home with you and see what you could do with it."

Tommy grinned again at that thought.

Skeeter set up the wastebasket and tossed the trash that had spilled back into it. Gilford came in a few minutes later, a slight smile on his face. For him, that was practically beaming.

"Crispin Loomis is a gambler," he said. "The Dallas police are quite familiar with him, although they've never been able to get enough evidence against him to arrest him."

Skeeter picked up her purse and started toward the door.

"Where are you going?" Gilford asked.

"No point in overlooking the obvious," Skeeter said. "I'm going to Boyd to see if the jerk's home."

On the way out the Jacksboro Highway, her anger was simmering just below the surface. She didn't know what she'd do if she confronted Frank Hobson. Trying to find him probably wasn't the smartest move she had ever made. Maybe she could talk to him, though, convince him that Tracy Roberts couldn't have had anything to do with Raider's death. He would have to look in other directions to find the dog's killer.

He could look toward Dallas and Crispin Loomis.

Loomis was a gambler, Gilford had said. And the beating Skeeter had witnessed in the Horsehead's parking lot had all the earmarks of what happened to somebody who welshed on a bet. Loomis had said, "Remember," as he ground his heel into the back of Hobson's hand. Definitely an object lesson.

Maybe Raider's death had been another reminder.

The more Skeeter thought about that, the more logical it seemed. Now all she had to do was find Hobson and get him to accept it and stay off Tracy Roberts's back.

She made good time, speeding but luckily avoiding any local cops or Wise County Sheriff's cars. It was a little before noon when she reached Boyd. She headed east on 114, found the cross street where the Hobsons lived, and turned onto it. She saw right away that the yellow Toyota pickup wasn't parked in front of the house. The carport at the side was empty, too.

And the BEWARE OF DOG sign was gone. Maybe Hobson's delicate nature couldn't stand to be reminded of Raider every time he saw it, Skeeter thought.

She parked and got out. No mention had been made of Hobson having another dog, but she checked the yard for fresh droppings before opening the gate. All the piles were old. She stepped inside the fence and started toward the house, leaving the gate open behind her this time.

Nobody answered the doorbell. Skeeter tried it several times, leaning on it for a good thirty seconds the last time. She rapped hard and loud on the door facing and called, "Mr. Hobson! Mrs. Hobson! Anybody home?"

Still no response. Skeeter sighed. She had been afraid of that. It was too early for Hobson to have gone to work at Lockheed. He was either out on some other errand—or holed up somewhere planning his revenge.

Laurie Hobson was a different matter. She was probably at her job. The woman across the street had said that Laurie worked at a beauty shop in Decatur, Skeeter remembered.

Decatur was only twelve or fourteen miles up the road. And how many beauty shops could a town of five thousand people have?

More than she would have hoped, she discovered when she borrowed a phone book at a convenience store on the edge of Decatur and checked the Yellow Page listings for beauty shops. She copied down the numbers of the shops in the book, got some change from the clerk who was about seventeen years old and a good eight months pregnant, then went outside to start making the calls. Each time one of the numbers answered, Skeeter asked simply, "Is Laurie there?" To the first six puzzled responses, she replied, "Sorry, guess I've got the wrong number," then hung up and dialed the next one on the list.

At the seventh shop, though, the woman who answered the phone said, "You mean Laurie Hobson?"

"That's right," Skeeter said, trying to sound casual. "She still works there, doesn't she?"

"Oh, yes, but she's gone to lunch. She ought to be back about one. Can I take a message for her?"

"No, thank you, ma'am. I'll give her a call back later." Skeeter hung up quickly before the lady could ask any more questions.

A glance at her watch told her it was only twelve-thirty. She spotted a restaurant down the street between a hardware store and a motel and decided to get something to eat.

The food was good enough she lingered over it a while and had a second glass of iced tea. As she paid her check and left, she asked the man at the cash register for directions to the street where the beauty shop that employed Laurie Hobson was located. The man pointed her toward the center of town.

Decatur wasn't very big; she could have driven the streets until she found what she was looking for. But asking saved some time and didn't cost anything. You didn't have to pay folks for information in a place like Decatur.

Less than five minutes later, she parked in front of a small brick building a block off the town square. A sign painted on the window read MOLLY'S BEAUTY SALON. She locked the pickup and went inside.

That unmistakable smell of permanent and hair spray hit her nose as she stepped in. To the left were three chairs facing a long mirror. A dryer was on the back wall, next to a door that led to a small office. There were a couple of wash bowls along the right wall, on the other side of a wrought iron and fake brick partition that created a small waiting area with chairs and magazines. Skeeter glanced at the selection: *Vogue, Elle, Redbook, Cosmopolitan, Field and Stream* . . . That last one must have snuck in from the barber shop down the block, she thought with a grin.

Laurie Hobson was working at the center chair on the left, combing out the wet hair of a middle-aged woman wearing a plastic smock. Without looking up from what she was doing, she said to Skeeter, "Just have a seat, ma'am. I'll be with you in a minute."

"No hurry," Skeeter said, sitting down in one of the chairs and reaching for the copy of *Field and Stream* out of sheer perversity. She wasn't really planning to read it anyway. As she held it up, she looked over the top of it and studied Laurie Hobson.

The woman looked like Skeeter remembered her—tall and slender, with brown hair parted in the middle and hanging straight to her shoulders. Her face was angular, the nose a little too sharp, and for somebody who worked in a beauty shop, her hair could have used some work. Maybe she was too busy fixing other people's hair and trying to make ends meet to worry about her own looks that much, Skeeter thought. Laurie wore jeans and a blue shirt with a short-sleeved white jacket over it.

As far as Skeeter could see, she and Laurie and the middle-aged customer were the only people in the shop. The door to the office was open, but nobody was in there. The woman Skeeter had talked to earlier must have left when Laurie came back from lunch.

"All right, Mrs. Kingsley, let's get you under the dryer now," Laurie said. She led the woman over to the big chair, settled the hood over her head, and turned on the machine.

Laurie came back around the partition, smiled at Skeeter, and said, "Now, what can I do for—" She broke off abruptly, the smile becoming a slight frown. "Don't I know you?"

"We haven't been introduced," Skeeter said as she tossed the magazine back onto the low table and stood up. "My name is Cassandra Barlow."

Laurie held a comb with a long, pointed handle. She wagged that handle at Skeeter like a finger and said, "I'm sure I've seen you before."

"You have. At your house in Boyd, a little over a week ago."

Eyes widening and fingers tightening on the comb, Laurie stared at Skeeter for a few seconds without saying anything. Then she hissed, "I knew it! You came there to see him! Didn't you?"

Frowning, Skeeter said, "I don't know what you mean, Mrs. Hobson. I was just talking to your husband about his dog—"

"You can't fool me." Laurie's head jerked from side to side. "I know all about Frank and his sluts. They say the wife's always the last one to know." A short, humorless bark of laughter erupted from her. "Not when her husband *brags* about it, she's not!"

Skeeter held up both hands, palms out, as Laurie took a step toward her. "Now, Mrs. Hobson—Laurie—you've got this all wrong," she said quickly. "I never even saw your husband until that Friday. All I wanted to talk to him about was the dog—"

Laurie glanced around, saw that the customer under the dryer wasn't paying any attention to the conversation, and moved another step closer to Skeeter. "The hell with the dog!" She sneered. "I guess you were too busy with Frank to ever get into that kind of animal training, weren't you? Why can't you tramps stick to your rich husbands and leave mine alone? Is that how you get your kicks? Taking everything away from a woman who don't have diddly-squat to start with?"

Skeeter felt her own anger starting to build. "Look, lady," she snapped, "I didn't come here to get insulted. I just want to know if you know where your husband is."

"You think I'd tell you if I knew?" Laurie had lowered her fists to her side. She moved them back and forth, the comb still clenched in the fingers of her right hand. Her voice shook with intensity but didn't rise over conversational levels as she said, "The hell I would! But it just so happens I *don't* know where he is. He didn't come home last night. I haven't seen him since he left yesterday afternoon to hang out with that friend of his—"

"Bobby Mack Wade?"

Laurie sneered again. "I should've figured that you'd know *him,* too. He probably bangs you when Frank's not around, doesn't he?"

Skeeter took a deep breath. "Lady, you have got it *all* wrong. I wouldn't fool around with your husband on a bet!"

That was the wrong thing to say and she knew it, but she was tired of Laurie Hobson yapping at her like Ida Lou Culbertson's little Chihuahua. Now, as Skeeter's words lashed at her, Laurie paled, shuddered, and then lunged forward, raking the point of the comb through the air toward Skeeter's face.

Skeeter dodged backward, hit the chair she had been sitting in earlier, and sat down again—hard—as she lost her balance. The low magazine table was between her and Laurie, and Laurie had to reach over it to jab the comb at her. That might have saved Skeeter from a nasty wound. Skeeter brought her feet up, planted them against the table, and shoved it forward as hard as she could. The opposite edge of it slammed into Laurie's shins.

Laurie let out a howl of pain. Skeeter came up out of the chair, knocked the comb out of the other woman's hand with a hard, slashing blow, then planted a hand on Laurie's shoulder and shoved. Laurie staggered backward and crashed against one of the operator's chairs. She fell but caught herself on the arm of the chair and hung there, breathing hard and glaring murderously at Skeeter.

"You are one crazy lady," Skeeter said as she glanced at the customer, who had finally noticed that something unusual was going on. The woman was gaping at Skeeter and Laurie. Skeeter shrugged and turned to walk out.

Laurie started to stand up and come after her. Skeeter heard the scrape of her feet against the tile floor and turned sharply, tensed to fight back if Laurie tried to jump her again. Laurie stopped instead and shouted, "You stay away from my husband, you hear! I'll kill you if you don't! I'll kill all of his sluts!"

Skeeter backed up to the door, opened it without taking her eyes off Laurie, then backed out. She didn't relax until she was in the pickup, pulling away from the curb.

And then a shudder ran through her as she glanced back and saw Laurie Hobson's hate-filled face staring at her through the glass of the beauty shop door.

Chapter Eleven

So that was Laurie Hobson. Sweet little Laurie.

Skeeter's jaw clenched as she drove down the highway from Decatur back toward Boyd. After that little encounter, she didn't have a whole lot of sympathy to spare for *either* of the Hobsons.

The whole situation left a bad taste in her mouth. She might go to the Horsehead tonight, she decided, even though it was one of her nights off, just to be able to sit with friends and drink some beer and try to forget.

But first she was going to swing back by the Hobson house and make sure Frank hadn't returned.

There were still no vehicles parked around the place when Skeeter pulled up. She got out of the pickup, opened the gate, and went up to the house. Ringing the doorbell got the same lack of response as earlier. Skeeter opened the screen door and rapped on the wooden one, then stood there on the porch listening to the silence.

She ought to get in her pickup and go back to Fort Worth, she knew. But she was remembering what Laurie had said about Hobson not coming home the night before. She had to find him and get him to listen to reason before he really hurt Tracy Roberts or somebody else.

Failing that, she'd stop him any way she could.

Maybe there was something in the house to indicate where he might be holed up. A pack of matches from a favorite bar, an address book, an ashtray filched from some motel . . . something. Skeeter didn't much like the idea of breaking and entering, but under the circumstances, she was willing to take the chance.

She walked around the house, being careful not to step in the piles of old dog droppings. She stopped and looked at the setup in the back yard. The chain-link fence ran all the way around the property, and about half the back yard was fenced off, too. The pen created by the fence had a large doghouse in it, empty now since Raider's death. Skeeter took a step toward it and saw the letters over the arching doorway of the doghouse. Not surprisingly, they spelled out Raider's name. They had been hand-painted, she saw as she came closer, and Hobson had done a meticulous job. The doghouse wasn't one of those prefabricated things you could buy at a lumber-yard and assemble yourself, either. It was built of plywood and good solid pine two-by-fours. The walls had exterior siding on them, and the roof was shingled. Skeeter leaned over and peered through the opening. She wasn't sure, but she thought the inside was carpeted.

Hobson had loved that dog, all right.

There were strips of rawhide and assorted chew toys scattered through the pen. Skeeter was surprised Hobson hadn't gotten rid of them, just like he had taken down the BEWARE OF DOG sign. Maybe he couldn't bring himself to go into the pen just yet.

The gate leading into the pen was wide open. Skeeter knew from frightening experience that Raider had had the run of the place most of the time. She guessed that the pen was here for the rare occasions when Hobson needed to shut the dog up. From the condition of the back yard—more toys, more droppings, bushes torn up, holes dug in the ground—Raider had spent more time there than he had in the pen.

There was a small patio with a sliding glass door leading into the house. Skeeter went over to it, grasped the handle, and rattled it. The door was loose in its tracks; it wouldn't be much of a chore to pop it open.

A faint noise made her stiffen suddenly. Unless she was badly mistaken, it had been the slamming of a car door out front.

Skeeter grimaced. With Frank Hobson already on a tear, there was no telling what he'd do if he found her nosing around his back yard.

So far no one had come around either corner of the house. She was still alone in the back yard. Maybe she could still get out of this. Maybe the car door she'd heard had been at a neighbor's house and she had panicked for nothing. Wasn't but one way to find out.

She started walking determinedly back around the house toward the front.

As she rounded the corner, she saw the red car parked behind her pickup. It was a two-door, low-slung foreign make, probably thirty or forty thousand dollars worth of automobile.

Nobody was in sight, but the front door of the house was open. Skeeter edged toward it. Hobson could have abandoned his Toyota, she supposed, and borrowed his girlfriend's car. Or the lady herself could have stopped by here looking for him, knowing that Laurie was at work in Decatur. The front door standing open like that meant whoever was here had a key. And they were probably wondering about that blue pickup parked in front of the house.

A woman appeared in the doorway before Skeeter could reach it. She stopped short and jumped a little as she saw Skeeter. "Oh, my goodness," Martina Danby said as she lifted a hand to her throat. "You scared me, Skeeter."

Glancing from Martina to the red car and back again, Skeeter said, "Is that yours?"

"Yes, it is. And I suppose that pickup is yours?"

Skeeter nodded.

"I didn't know who might be here," Martina went on. "I was looking for Frank."

"He's not here."

"I can see that." Martina's voice was more cool and assured now that she was over her brief fright. She was wearing a short brown leather skirt that showed off her legs and a lightweight fur jacket over a green silk blouse. She brushed back her long hair and went on, "What are you doing here?"

"Same as you," Skeeter replied bluntly. "Looking for Frank. Only I don't have a key."

Martina gave her a slight smile and said, "Maybe he just hasn't gotten around to giving you one yet. He sometimes waits until a girl . . . proves herself, let's say . . . before he gives her a key."

"You're taking this mighty cool."

Martina shrugged. "I don't see any reason to be upset. It's hardly like either Frank or I could demand fidelity from each other, is it?"

"Reckon not. But maybe you're jumping to conclusions. I came to see the man about a dog."

With a laugh, Martina shook her head. "I can't imagine Frank passing up something like you, Skeeter. I mean, you're just his type."

Skeeter swallowed the anger she felt welling up her throat. Calling her Frank Hobson's type was just about the lowest insult Martina could have come up with. But Skeeter's brain was working along with her emotions, and she realized that Martina had no idea Hobson had discovered she was a P.I.

"Well, hon, I reckon we've all made our mistakes where men are concerned," she said.

105

Martina laughed again. "Amen to that. But don't tell Frank I said it."

"Don't worry, I won't." Skeeter hesitated, then asked, "Do you have any idea where he might be?"

"I have no idea at all. When I saw you, I hoped you might know. You see, we were supposed to . . . get together last night, but Frank stormed away from the ranch for some reason. He didn't even tell Roy or me that he was leaving. Bobby Mack tried to find out what was wrong, but all Frank would tell him was that he was going to even the score for Raider." Martina grimaced and pushed her hair back again. "Don't tell Frank this, either, but I never liked that dog. I always made Frank pen him up when I came to visit. That's why I liked this place better than that trailer house. The pen here was so much sturdier. I sometimes had nightmares that Raider would get loose while Frank and I were in bed together and come in the house and attack me and rip me to shreds in some sort of jealous rage. It was horrible . . . Am I disturbing you, Skeeter?"

"Are you trying to?"

"Of course not."

"Just seems to me you might've been more worried about Frank's wife catching you than his dog."

"No, I never worried about Laurie," Martina said, shaking her head. "We were always very careful."

This was the strangest conversation to be having in somebody's front yard in the middle of the afternoon, Skeeter thought. Somehow, she wasn't surprised that Hobson and Martina Danby had been having an affair, as ill-matched as they appeared to be on the surface. Martina probably had a whole flock of blue-collar sexual fantasies.

"He ever take you to a motel?" Skeeter asked. If Hobson had used one particular place for his rendezvouses with

Martina, maybe he had gone to ground there now.

"No, I always came to wherever he was living at the time."

Skeeter inclined her head toward the house. "Not a very fancy place."

"It's an absolute hovel. Laurie's a terrible housekeeper, I'm afraid, to go along with being a shrew. But I didn't mind. The mess even added something to the ambiance at times."

Yep, Skeeter decided, this was one sick relationship she'd stumbled on. And she'd had about enough of it.

"If you see Frank, tell him I'm looking for him, okay?"

"I'd be glad to," Martina said with all the graciousness of a hostess in her own home. "Is there any other message you'd like for me to give him?"

Skeeter shook her head. No point in getting Martina any more involved than she already was. "I'd better get going."

"Me, too." Martina turned toward the door. "I'll lock up, since you don't have a key."

Skeeter couldn't decide if that sweet-voiced comment was another dig or not, and she didn't care. More than ever, all she wanted was to get out of here. And she hoped that once she was gone, she never saw the place again.

Chapter Twelve

She halfway expected Hobson to have come back to the agency looking for her, but when she got there, everything was peaceful. The first thing she did was call Tracy Roberts.

An answering machine picked up after the fourth ring. While Skeeter was leaving a message the line clicked.

"It's you," the woman said. "I was afraid it might be—"

"I know," Skeeter cut in. "I was afraid something had happened to you."

"We stopped answering the phone and let the machine pick it up. That man has called and threatened us several times today. We're leaving while we still have a chance."

"That's a good idea," Skeeter said. "Fact is, I was going to suggest that when I tried to get in touch with you. Where are you going?"

Tracy Roberts hesitated before replying, as if afraid to even speak the words. "We have an aunt and uncle in Brownwood," she finally said. "I think we'll be safe there. I hope so."

"Can you give me a number where you can be reached?" Skeeter asked.

Tracy hesitated again before giving her the number. She requested that Skeeter not write down her name with the number. She didn't want Hobson having any chance of finding her. Skeeter gave her word before hanging up.

Skeeter looked out the window scanning the sprawling city, its lights beginning to twinkle in the hazy dusk. Somewhere out there was Frank Hobson, and he was going to be

108

disappointed that Tracy Roberts was gone. That would mean he'd have to find a new target for his rage.

Skeeter had a pretty good idea who that was going to be.

She didn't know if Hobson had gotten her home address when he broke into the agency, but chances were he knew her real name now; the vice cops had probably told him that along with the fact she was a P.I. She had already stopped at the Westside video store to warn Rita. Rita had thought it was a good time to go visit her cousin Annelle in Arlington and warned Skeeter to be careful.

Skeeter's hands tightened on the steering wheel as she approached their house, she scanned the cars parked along the curb. The streetlights had come on as night fell, and there was plenty of light to see the vehicles. No sign of a yellow Toyota. Skeeter wheeled into the driveway, killed the engine, and got out.

A little shiver ran through her as she walked toward the front door. Just the chill in the air she told herself.

She unlocked the door and stepped in and wrinkled her nose at the smell that hit her. Must be a sewer problem, she thought. She reached out to flick the light switch in the hall, then jerked her hand back from what she touched.

She started to utter an exclamation of surprise, then decided it would be too appropriate under these circumstances. She made another try for the light switch, got it this time, and blinked as the bright illumination came on.

The streaks of manure that had been smeared on the wall continued on into the living room and beyond to the kitchen. Skeeter could see that far. She couldn't see into the kitchen itself, just the wall beside the entrance, and she couldn't see into either bedroom. Hobson could still be in the house.

She didn't doubt for an instant that he was responsible for

this degradation. Furniture was overturned and broken and slashed, the chaos remindful of what he had done to the office, only worse. He hadn't been looking for information here. This was destruction for the sake of destruction.

Skeeter's pulse hammered heavily in her head. She was mad and scared at the same time, unsure which emotion was the stronger.

The door of the hall closet was close at hand. Skeeter opened it quietly and felt on top of the shelf. Nothing seemed to be out of place in the closet, and when her fingers reached behind a couple of old-fashioned hatboxes and closed over the butt of the .38, she knew Hobson hadn't bothered looking in here. A box of bullets was stuck on another shelf, behind a Monopoly game. Just your usual hall closet sort of stuff, Skeeter thought as she thumbed cartridges into the revolver.

When the gun was loaded, she moved on through the living room into the kitchen, snapping on lights as she went. The kitchen was empty, but Hobson had been there. He had been in the bedrooms, too, still wreaking his havoc. Skeeter moved carefully into her room, wincing at the destruction. She blinked rapidly and felt tears welling up in her eyes as she saw how the stuffed 'possum she kept on her bed had been shredded. Stink had been Doug's favorite animal when they were all still together, but when he and his older brother had moved to Houston to be with their dad, he had left the 'possum with Skeeter. "So you won't be alone, Mama," he had said. Now as she looked at what remained of the toy, her throat felt so tight it was like someone choking her.

Hobson was gone, Skeeter concluded after ten nervous minutes of searching the house. Gone but not forgotten. Not hardly.

It would take a long time to clean up this mess and put things back in order.

First, she called the video store. When Rita answered, Skeeter said, "Don't come back here, kid. It's time to go visit your cousin Annelle in Arlington. Hobson's been here and he trashed the place. He might come back."

"Are you all right, Skeeter?"

"Yeah. Shaken up a little. I'm leaving right now."

"Shouldn't you call the police?"

"I'll call 'em from the club."

"This is really bad, isn't it?"

"And getting worse," Skeeter said.

Jasper took one look at her and said, "What's wrong, girl?"

"Every blasted thing you can think of." Skeeter edged her rump onto a stool and sighed. The mournful ballad coming from the jukebox suited her mood perfectly. She went on, "There's a crazy man after me."

Quickly, she filled him in on what had been happening, and Jasper's face grew more solemn and concerned as she talked. When she was finished, he said, "I saw you talkin' on the pay phone when you came in. You call the cops?"

"Yeah. I got hold of a detective lieutenant I know. He was going to do what he can—which ain't going to be a heck of a lot. Give me a beer."

Jasper handed her a longneck. "You'll need a place to stay tonight."

She looked at him with a wry grin. "You offering?"

"Yeah. As a friend, Skeeter. You know that."

"Yeah. I guess I do."

"You got anything else in mind, there's a fella over there who'd be happy to oblige, I reckon." Jasper nodded toward the other side of the room.

Skeeter turned on the barstool and saw Buck Ngyuen sitting at one of the tables. He gave her a big grin and stood up.

He was wearing his usual Stetson and jeans, and a purple Western shirt with white piping.

"Howdy, cowboy," Skeeter said as he stepped up to the bar. "Haven't seen you in a while."

"I've been busy ridin' herd on them dang computers," Buck said. "We're puttin' in a new system at the office." He frowned, "Something wrong? Shoot, tell me all about it, Skeeter."

She glanced at Jasper. She'd already gone through the whole story once for him, and she didn't much feel like telling it again. But Buck was looking at her with such a concerned expression on his face, she couldn't just brush him off.

"Well, it all started with this man and his dog . . ."

When she'd spun the yarn again, Buck looked even more worried than Jasper had. "There must be somethin' we can do about this loco hombre," he said, the B-Western dialogue sounding completely serious even if it was coming out of an oriental face. " 'Bout time we had us a showdown with that no-good jasper—"

"Watch it, son," Jasper said.

"No-good ranny?"

"That's better."

"If you two are through," Skeeter said, "I just thought I'd remind you that I have a real-life lunatic after me."

Jasper shook his head. "This fella Hobson don't sound crazy to me, Skeeter. He sounds *mean*."

"You could be right."

Buck leaned forward and took her hand. "You can't go back to your place tonight, Skeeter," he said. "Why don't you come home with me? I'll protect you."

Skeeter looked at him and smiled. "How much do you weigh, Buck?"

He frowned in surprise at the question. "Around one-forty, I guess."

"And you told me that you don't know the martial arts."

"Well, I just never got around to practicing them enough—"

"And those jeans are too tight for you to be hiding a hogleg in there."

"You mean a gun? I've never used one. But I've seen a lot of movies—"

Skeeter made her voice hard. "So you want me to stake my life on a skinny, clumsy computer nerd who likes to play cowboy."

Hurt flared in Buck's eyes. One hand gripped the edge of the bar very tightly. "You got no right—" he began.

"I got the best right in the world, hon," Skeeter said sharply. "I'm trying to watch out for me. I can't baby-sit you at the same time."

His head jerked up and down in an oddly formal nod. "All right. If that is the way you wish it."

"Better watch it, Hopalong. Your accent's slipping."

Buck turned and stalked away, his spine stiff. He didn't look back as he went to the jukebox, fed in some quarters, and pushed several buttons. He stayed there, leaning on the brightly lit music machine, palms flat against the clear plastic cover.

Jasper leaned forward and rasped in a whisper, "What'd you do *that* for? You destroyed that kid!"

Sadly, Skeeter looked up at him. "You said it yourself, Jasper. He's a kid."

Jasper just stared at her for a moment, understanding seeping into his brain. Finally he nodded and said, "Oh. Yeah. But do you think he understands?"

"Not right now. But when he thinks about it, maybe he will."

Skeeter glanced at Buck again. He left the jukebox, went

back to a table, and ordered another drink.

He stayed there all through the evening. Monday nights were slow, so Jasper was able to stay close to Skeeter most of the time. Although they talked about it at length, neither of them came up with anything else they could do to rein in Frank Hobson. Skeeter wasn't even sure any longer if it would do any good to find out who had killed Raider. Hobson was too far out over the edge.

By midnight, the thick haze of smoke in the room and the beers she had drunk were getting to be too much for Skeeter. She pushed herself up off the stool and said, "I'm going to go to the ladies' room, then get some fresh air."

"You sure that's a good idea?" Jasper asked with a frown.

"Sounds like a heck of a good idea to me."

"I'm talking about going outside. Hobson's seen you here before. He could be waiting around somewhere close by."

"I'm not leaving. Not even going in the parking lot. I just want to step out the door for a minute."

Jasper looked around. "Chuckie's on a break. Wait until he gets back out here and I'll go with you."

"To the ladies' room?"

"Dammit, Skeeter, quit bein' funny. You know what I mean."

And here she'd thought she was being pretty humorous. Must be the beer, she decided. It was affecting her more than usual, probably because she was tired from the long day and under a heck of a strain to boot. She waved a hand in surrender. "All right, all right. I'll go ahead and tinkle, then wait for you to catch up before I go outside."

"Thank you," Jasper said solemnly.

She turned and stepped down off the deck in front of the bar, stumbling just slightly as she did so. Still, the slip was enough to make her stop and mutter, "I'm drunk!" She sounded astonished by the realization. With a shake of her head, she made her way toward the restrooms.

When she came out and glanced toward the bar, she saw that Chuckie still hadn't returned from his break and that Jasper had gotten busier with the customers. There was no extra bartender, not on a Monday. Jasper wasn't even looking in her direction.

No reason for him to act like such a mama hen, Skeeter thought. All she wanted to do was stick her head out the front door for a few seconds. People were coming and going all the time. What did he think was going to happen to her? Even Hobson, crazy as he was, wouldn't try to jump her under such circumstances.

Skeeter walked toward the door.

On the way she had to pass Buck Ngyuen's table, but she didn't look at him. He was probably still mad at her, and she couldn't blame him. After all, she had been trying to get him mad. Easiest way to keep him out of trouble.

She pushed open the entrance door and stepped out, drawing a deep breath of the cold night air into her lungs as she let the door swing shut behind her. She glanced to the south, across the river, and saw the lights of downtown, little yellow squares dotting the darkness here and there in the windows of the skyscrapers. Skeeter took another deep breath, looked the other way, and saw Frank Hobson coming at her, a knife in his hand.

Chapter Thirteen

Nothing like a crazy man trying to kill you to sober you up in a hurry, Skeeter realized as she ducked under the blade and dove for Hobson's legs. She slammed into them, rolling and going for his knees like an offensive lineman playing dirty. Hobson didn't fall, though. He staggered, leaned over, jabbed the knife at her again. Skeeter barely twisted out of the way and scrambled to her feet.

She ought to be screaming for help, but she didn't have enough breath for that. It was all she could do to stay out of his way as he came toward her again, swinging wildly with the knife.

The .38 was still in her purse, but there was no time to stop and dig it out. She did the next best thing, dodging one of Hobson's thrusts, shifting her grip on the purse's strap, and whipping it toward his head. The bag cracked against his skull just above the ear, making him stumble again.

Skeeter gasped for air and caught him one more time on the backswing. When she tried again he flung up his free arm and let the gun-weighted purse wrap the strap around his wrist. He jerked it viciously away from Skeeter and flung it into the parking lot.

Her eyes flicked after the purse for a split-second. Beyond it, she saw lights pulling into the lot. No time for anything else to register. Hobson was still trying to carve her up. She ducked back out of his reach, but he came after her. The high-heeled boots Skeeter wore weren't made for fancy footwork. She felt one of the heels suddenly snap off, and she lurched to one side, her balance going. She fell on the edge of the parking lot.

Hobson raised the knife and came after her.

The door of the club flew open and Buck Ngyuen crashed into Hobson's back. Both men spilled to the ground. The knife clattered away from Hobson.

With a roar, he rolled over, came up on his knees, and backhanded Buck just as he was trying to struggle to his feet. Buck went sprawling again, and Hobson looked around wildly for Skeeter. At that moment, the headlights from the parking lot speared him.

Skeeter knew she would never forget how he looked at that moment. His pants were stained with grease, and the tails of his flannel shirt flopped over his belt. Several days' worth of grizzled beard stubble dotted his jowls, and his hair was a wild tangle. He had one arm flung up trying to block the lights, and as he squinted past it, Skeeter could see the madness in his gaze. He stumbled forward a couple of steps.

Car doors slammed. Skeeter heard footsteps running toward her, and a strangely familiar voice yelled, "There he is! Get him!" Hobson turned and ran toward the corner of the club.

He disappeared around the corner of the building with a couple of bulky shapes pounding after him. More footsteps came up to Skeeter, and a hand took her arm and lifted her to her feet with surprising ease considering the slender build of its owner. Crispin Loomis asked, "Are you all right, my dear?"

Skeeter took a couple of deep breaths and then managed to nod. She said shakily, "I . . . I'm fine. But what about Buck?"

"Your gallant cowboy?" Loomis asked. "I'll see to him. Are you sure you're all right?"

"Yeah. See about Buck."

Loomis let go of her arm and trotted over to Buck's side. Skeeter followed Loomis. The young man was still stretched out on the asphalt, but he was moving around, mostly twisting his head from side to side and moaning occasionally. Kneeling beside him, the Englishman studied him for a moment and then said, "I think he'll be all right. He just got his bell rung, as you Americans say." Loomis slipped an arm under Buck's shoulders and lifted him into a sitting position.

"I'd better call an ambulance," Skeeter said.

"Probably not necessary," Loomis replied. He asked Buck, "Are you all right?"

Buck lifted a hand to his head and moaned again. Thickly, he said, "Yeah . . . Yeah, I'm . . . all right."

"Where are you? Do you know?"

"Saigon . . . ? No, that's not right. Fort Worth! I'm in Fort Worth."

"Very good. Do you know your name?"

"Buck . . ."

"Excellent. Now, how many fingers?" Loomis held up two in front of Buck's face.

Buck said in a stronger voice, "Two. And I know what you're doing, mister. I don't have a concussion."

"No, I don't believe you do, my friend. Would you like to stand up?"

"Yeah." Buck looked up at Skeeter, his face creasing in concern. "Skeeter! You okay?"

She nodded. "Yeah, I'm fine, thanks to you, Buck."

Together, she and Loomis lifted Buck to his feet. He wobbled for a few seconds, then steadied. He muttered, "I'm glad I came after you to apologize, Skeeter."

"Apologize? To me? After the things I said to you?"

Buck grinned sheepishly. "Ah, heck, I knew you were just

tryin' to protect me. You think I'm just a dumb kid."

"Well, I reckon I was wrong about that," Skeeter said softly.

Several people came out of the club, looked at them strangely, then went on to their car. The commotion probably hadn't been heard over the wailing of the jukebox inside, Skeeter realized. Jasper had probably thought she was still in the restroom.

Loomis's two companions came back around the building, puffing heavily. One of them shook his head as they came up to Loomis, Buck, and Skeeter. "The guy got away," he said breathlessly. "He can run like a rabbit for a big guy."

"I'm sure we'll catch up with Mr. Hobson later," Loomis said, an icy tone creeping into his voice. "Right now I'm worried about this lady and her friend."

Loomis was smooth, all right, Skeeter thought. Her brain was starting to work again, and she remembered what Lars Gilford had told her about this Englishman whose home was now Dallas. Loomis was in his late thirties and handsome, even though he was lean almost to the point of gauntness. His suit and shoes were expensive. Only the best for Crispin Loomis.

Jasper poked his head out the door, his eyes getting wide as he saw the little group gathered there in front of the club. "Skeeter!" he exclaimed. "What happened?"

"Buck and I had a little run-in with Hobson, but these fellas helped us out." She took Buck's arm and steered him toward the door. "I think you ought to take Buck in the back room and get him to lie down and take it easy."

"No, Skeeter," Buck protested. "I want to stay with—"

Ignoring his words, Skeeter handed him over to Jasper and said firmly, "Please."

Jasper glanced at Loomis and the others. "You sure about this, Skeeter?" He sounded definitely dubious.

"I'm sure," she told him.

"All right. But I'll be back in a minute." He took Buck's arm and led the young man into the club.

Skeeter turned back to the Englishman and said, "Look, I'm going to talk plain, Mr. Loomis."

He raised one perfectly arched eyebrow. "You know who I am."

"Yeah, I know a lot. I know that you've got a grudge against Frank Hobson. So do I."

"I wouldn't call it a grudge. The man owes me a great deal of money. I just want him to pay me what he owes." Loomis sighed. "I doubt he's going to be able to, since he's spending his time attacking lovely young women."

Skeeter ignored the compliment. "He's mad because somebody killed his dog. You wouldn't know anything about that, would you, Mr. Loomis?"

The two men with Loomis frowned darkly at her, but the Englishman just laughed. "Hardly. I'd had no reason to harm that animal, Miss . . . ?"

"Barlow. My friends call me Skeeter."

"Very well then, Skeeter. All I want is my money, and Hobson is a great deal less likely to have it now that the dog is dead. Even ten percent of Raider's winnings were better than nothing."

Skeeter shook her head. "Ten percent? You mean you were taking ninety percent of what Raider won?"

"Not at all. Ten percent was Hobson's share, and he in turn would pay that to me—if he knew what was good for him. He didn't, always. His partners got the other ninety percent."

"Partners?"

"Roy Danby and Bobby Mack Wade. They really owned the animal, you see."

Skeeter didn't, and Loomis must have seen the confusion on her face, because he went on, "The dog belonged to Hobson at first, I believe, but I'm not the only one he wagered with. Our association is relatively recent. Before that, he bet with Danby and Wade."

"And when they won and Hobson couldn't pay them, they took shares of the dog instead." Skeeter nodded, beginning to understand now.

"Exactly. It was like owning a piece of a prizefighter. Hobson got to keep the dog, since he was so devoted to it and it responded so well to him, but most of Raider's winnings went straight into the pockets of Danby and Wade, and they made the decisions about who the dog fought." Loomis smiled at her. "You obviously know these people and understand what I'm talking about, and I'm wondering how that is."

She told him, "I've been to the Rising Star Ranch."

"Ah! I've heard of it, of course, but never actually attended one of the exhibitions."

"You haven't missed a heck of a lot," Skeeter told him bluntly.

A few more things were making sense now. She could understand how Hobson had been able to hire a high-powered attorney to keep Raider from being destroyed after the attack on Joey. Roy Danby and Bobby Mack Wade had paid for the lawyer. They had a bigger stake in Raider's continued good health than Hobson did. Hobson probably hadn't told anyone that the other two men actually owned the dog, not even Laurie, so he'd had to make it look like he was still in charge and taking care of everything. His pride demanded that much.

Skeeter looked up at Loomis and asked, "How's Hobson going to pay you now that Raider's dead?"

Loomis shrugged elegant shoulders. "That's his problem."

"And if he doesn't pay you, you'll kill him?"

The other two men looked uneasy, but Loomis took it all in stride. "I'll convince him that he made a very serious error by incurring such a debt in the first place," he said. "You can read into that whatever you'd like, Miss Barlow."

A part of Skeeter wanted to tell him to hurry up and catch Hobson and kill him like the cockroach he was. She couldn't do that, though. She was a respectable citizen or at least tried to be.

"Look," she said, "I appreciate the help. I'd probably be dead now if you hadn't showed up."

"A lucky circumstance for us all. I remembered that Hobson had frequented this establishment before and decided to look for him here again."

"Anyway, like I said, thanks for helping. But I'm out of this now. I can't help you find Hobson or anything like that."

"Of course not. I wouldn't dream of putting you in an awkward position, Miss Barlow. But I am curious about why Hobson has launched this vendetta against you."

Skeeter shrugged. "He thinks I helped somebody kill his dog. He's wrong, but he hasn't been standing still long enough for anybody to convince him otherwise. The last thirty-six hours or so, he's been going around making a major nuisance of himself."

"Well, we shall see what can be done about that." Loomis looked over his shoulder at his burly companions. "Come along, gentlemen. Good night, Miss Barlow. Do you need an escort home?"

Skeeter glanced at the door of the club and saw that it had

opened. Jasper was leaning against one side of it. "No," she said with a smile. "I've already got somebody to take me home."

"Very well, then. Good night again." Loomis strolled back to his car, the other two men following him.

Skeeter watched them go, then turned back to Jasper. He said, "You know, you do some damn stupid things when you drink too much."

"So I've been told," she sighed. She rubbed one hand over her backside. It was aching pretty good from tumbling around on the asphalt. "I'll come back inside and be good."

"All right. Buck's okay, by the way. He's spoutin' lines from old Roy Rogers movies at Chuckie." Jasper grinned. "Boy does a pretty good Gabby Hayes. You ought to hear it."

"I'm sure I will," Skeeter said.

Weariness settled in as she sat at the bar. After seeing how exhausted she was, Jasper said, "Chuckie, you're closin' on your own."

"Sure, Jasper," Chuckie said. "Skeeter, you okay?"

"I will be," she told him, "soon's I get about a week's sleep."

"Better go get started on it, then."

She nodded and picked up the purse she'd retrieved from the parking lot. The weight of the .38 pulled at her shoulder as she slung the purse over it. She leaned over and kissed Buck lightly on the cheek. "Thanks, cowboy."

He thumbed his hat to the back of his head and looked embarrassed. "Shucks, ma'am, 'tweren't nothin'."

Skeeter put her arms around his neck, leaned in closer to him, and said, "Buck, I really appreciate what you did, but . . . get a life."

He grinned. "That'd be the easy way, but it wouldn't be—"

"The cowboy way." Skeeter, Jasper, and Chuckie all said the Riders in the Sky catch-phrase together with him, then Skeeter waved and walked out with Jasper.

"Your truck or my van?" he asked.

"Better take 'em both," Skeeter said. "Wouldn't want to leave either one of them here overnight."

"You're probably right. You can follow me back to my place."

"Sure. You know, Jasper, I'm not even sure where you live."

"It's a long way out on El Campo. Not far from your part of town."

She nodded. "Think we could swing by my house first? I know it's a little out of the way, but I've been in these clothes all day and I'd sure like to pick up a few things. I was too shook up when I was there earlier to do anything except get out."

Jasper considered, then said, "Sure. Just keep an eye out for Hobson."

"Always."

She unlocked the pickup and gave Jasper a lift around to the back of the building to get his van.

A little shudder ran through her. She'd come close tonight, closer than she'd ever come. She didn't know if Hobson was already aware that Tracy Roberts, her sister, and her nephew had left town. Skeeter wasn't sure if it even mattered now. Hobson would be after anybody he thought had ever crossed him.

She wondered if he had a list. Crazies sometimes did. If Frank Hobson had made a list of his enemies, who would be on it? His wife? Roy Danby and Bobby Mack Wade, the men who had taken ownership of his beloved Raider away from him? Crispin Loomis? How many other people who had been unlucky enough to cross his path?

Jasper had said that Hobson might not be crazy, just mean. That was wrong. He was *both.*

From the window of his van, Jasper waved for Skeeter to take the lead. She did so, knowing that they would switch places once they'd stopped by her house. Chances were Hobson wouldn't have gone back there again tonight, but you never could tell what somebody like that would do. Skeeter was mighty glad she was going to have Jasper with her.

She felt a little warm glow inside when she thought about Jasper, and it was followed by a tingle of anticipation. She didn't know what would happen when they got to his house, and she was willing to bet he wasn't sure, either. Yeah, he'd invited her as a friend, even made a point of saying that. Skeeter's lips curved in a slight smile. Yeah, right. They were just friends, but nothing said friends couldn't do a little romping together in the sack. Jasper was older, but he was sort of sexy in a weatherbeaten way.

Besides, after everything that had happened today, she could really use somebody to hold her for a while.

"You are getting way ahead of yourself, girl," she said out loud as she sent the truck up the entrance ramp from Forest Park Boulevard to the West Freeway. Traffic at this time of night wasn't too bad on the freeway, and they made good time. Her house was located in a nice middle-class residential neighborhood. Most of the houses were at least twenty years old, and Skeeter's was even older than that. But she liked it, liked the big trees in the front yard and the good-sized back yard.

She made the turn onto the cross street where she lived. Her foot jerked instinctively to the brake pedal as the head-lights washed over an old yellow Toyota pickup parked at the curb in front of the house. Skeeter veered her truck sharply toward the opposite curb, glad there was no other traffic on the road. Her heart pounded heavily in her chest as she brought the pickup to a stop.

Jasper pulled his van up behind her and cut the lights. Skeeter forced her brain to work. Jasper didn't know which house was hers, and he might not have noticed the Toyota. He probably thought she was just stopping to go in the house as planned.

She turned off her own lights and killed the motor, then reached up and popped the cover off the dome light. It took only a second to twist the bulb and pull it loose from the socket. She dropped it on the floorboard on the passenger side, then eased the door open and slipped out. Jasper still had his engine idling behind her pickup.

Skeeter ducked down and ran along the bed of the truck, using it to shield her from view. Jasper rolled down his window as she came up to the van. In a low voice, he asked, "Something wrong?"

"That's Hobson's pickup," Skeeter hissed, pointing through the van windshield. Jasper tensed and snapped his head around to look.

After a few seconds, he said, "Don't see anybody movin' around over there. Everything's dark."

That was true. The whole neighborhood was dark and quiet, asleep just like it ought to be. Weren't even any dogs barking.

"That's my place he's parked in front of," Skeeter said. "Could be he's inside, waiting for me or Rita to come home."

"Well, then, let's call the cops."

Jasper's suggestion made sense. Hobson was somewhere in the area, that was for sure. If they could disable his pickup and then call the police, he wouldn't be able to get away.

"All right, but let's let the air out of his tires first."

"What? What the hell are you talkin' about, Skeeter?"

"I don't want him getting away this time," she said fervently. "That jerk has caused enough trouble, Jasper. He violated my home. He's got to be stopped. Let's sneak over there, let the air out of his tires, and then you can go call the cops while I keep an eye on the place."

Jasper sighed. "I guess I see your point, but you got it backwards. You'll go call the cops and I'll stay."

"Whatever. Let's just do it."

Skeeter was operating on adrenaline now, her weariness chased away by anger and righteous indignation. Jasper started to open the door of his van, but she tapped him on the shoulder and pointed to the dome light. He nodded and took the bulb out, then joined her on the sidewalk. They catfooted around to the back of his van.

"Gonna have to get across the street," he whispered.

"Duck down and go in a hurry."

She took off first, running across the street in a crouch. Jasper followed right behind her, and as they reached the cover of another parked car, he knelt, held onto the vehicle's rear bumper for support, and hissed, "I feel like a damn fool."

"Better that than dead," Skeeter told him, and he inclined his head in acknowledgment of her point. She raised up a little and peered through the front and back windshields of the car they were using for cover. "Oh, no!"

"What is it?"

"He's in there."

"In the pickup?"

Skeeter nodded and looked again. Enough illumination came from a streetlight down the block for her to see the silhouette of Frank Hobson's head through the back window of the Toyota. "He's just sitting there."

"Wouldn't he have noticed us pull up across the street?"

"Maybe he thought we live over there and didn't pay much attention."

"I thought he knows what your pickup looks like."

That was right, Skeeter thought. Her brain wasn't working at top speed tonight. Anybody as paranoid as Hobson would have certainly looked around when two vehicles pulled up near where he was staking out his quarry's house. And he probably would have recognized her truck, even if it was too dark to really make out the color of it. Now, as she watched him, she realized something else was wrong.

"Jasper, since I've been watching him, he hasn't moved. Not an inch. He's just sitting there, sort of leaning against the door."

"Maybe he's asleep," Jasper suggested.

Skeeter straightened. "I'm going to find out."

"Blast it, come back here!" Jasper whispered urgently, grabbing at her sleeve. He was too slow, and she walked boldly along the curb toward the Toyota, angling across behind it to come up beside the driver's door. Jasper hurried after her. Wasn't much point in stealth now.

Skeeter slipped her hand into her purse and closed her fingers around the butt of the .38. Her anger was almost totally in control of her. If Hobson was asleep, he was going to wake up with the barrel of a gun kissing his nose. Maybe like Buck, she'd been watching too many movies, but damn! —it would feel good to throw down on the creep and hold him at gunpoint until the cops got there.

She pulled the gun out of her purse and reached for the door handle with the other hand. Moving smoothly and efficiently, she jerked the door open and then lifted the .38, bringing it to bear on Hobson.

"Don't move!"

He ignored the command, swaying toward her. In the light from the streetlamp, Skeeter saw the blank look on his face, in profile toward her. She saw the little black hole in the left side of his head, and as he flopped halfway out of the truck, held in only by his seat belt, she saw the mess where the bullet had come out, taking a big chunk of the right side of his skull with it. Skeeter just stared as Jasper came up beside her and said, "Good Lord! He's dead!"

Skeeter slowly lowered the gun. She wouldn't be needing it anymore.

Chapter Fourteen

She was glad she had been with other people all night and could prove it, because the hole in Frank Hobson's head had been put there by a slug from a .38—just like the one in Skeeter's purse. At least that's what the cops thought, judging by the size of the entrance wound. They hadn't recovered the bullet yet, so they couldn't run a ballistics check and totally eliminate her gun as the murder weapon. She had a feeling that none of the cops took her seriously as a suspect, though, not after talking to Jasper, Buck, and Chuckie.

But even if she wasn't a suspect, she could tell that they weren't real happy with her. As she sat in an uncomfortable metal chair in front of an equally austere metal desk in a room in White Settlement police headquarters, she glanced at her watch. Four in the morning, she thought. She didn't know what was holding her up.

On the other side of the desk, a detective named Harkness was staring at the notes he had made on a yellow legal pad. He looked even more tired than Skeeter felt. She knew Harkness by reputation, although they'd never met, and she knew he was a good, honest cop.

"All right, Ms. Barlow," he finally said. "It seems like we've covered everything—"

"Twice," Skeeter put in.

Harkness's mouth twitched a little, like he couldn't decide whether to grin or look annoyed at her comment. He didn't do either one, just went on, "And I suppose we can let you go now. The department appreciates your cooperation."

"Always glad to help," Skeeter said, and even she didn't know if she was being sarcastic or not. She pushed back the chair and started to stand up.

"Just one more thing," Harkness said, and Skeeter hoped desperately that he wasn't one of those cops who'd seen every episode of "Columbo" ever made. He went on, "Do you have any idea where we can find this man Loomis?"

She'd had to give them Loomis; after all, who was more likely to have blown Hobson's brains out than the British gambler or one of his flunkys? She said, "I reckon you can find somebody on the Dallas force who can help you out. They know him over there. Like I said, he lives there. Doesn't stop him from doing business on this side of 360." The highway she mentioned ran north and south through Arlington, effectively dividing Fort Worth's sphere of influence from Dallas's.

"Okay," Harkness grunted. "Thanks again."

This time he let her get out of the office. As she stepped into the hallway, Jasper rose from the chair where he had been waiting. There were trenches of strain in his lean cheeks as he looked at her. "You all right?" he asked.

"I reckon I'm okay," she replied.

"They let you go?"

"No reason not to. It's pretty obvious they don't think either one of us killed Hobson."

Jasper smiled. "I wouldn't say that. Fella I talked to seemed to have it figured that we were in on it together."

Skeeter blinked at him in surprise. "How could they think that? My gun hadn't even been fired."

"Hobson had been dead for a little while before we found him. There was time to clean and reload the gun."

"Now that's just crazy, we would have just gotten rid of the gun if we'd done something like that. I wanted Hobson stopped, but I wouldn't have killed him."

Even as she spoke, Skeeter had to admit, deep inside her, that she didn't know if she was telling the truth. She had been mad enough at Hobson to shoot him when he was trying to slice her up. But to shoot a man through the head at pointblank range, in cold blood . . .

There was no doubt about the pointblank part. The powder burns around the entrance wound showed that the gun had been held, if not directly against Hobson's head, at least within an inch or two. Both windows in the Toyota had been rolled down to let in the cool night air. Somebody had walked up to Hobson and shot him, simple as that, the bullet passing through his head and going out the other window. Either the killer was somebody he knew and trusted, or else he had been asleep while the killer slipped up on him.

She and Jasper started down the hall toward the front of the building. The door of one of the offices on the right side of the corridor opened, and three men stepped out. Skeeter recognized one of them as the detective who had interrogated Jasper earlier. She knew the other men, too.

The two vice cops from the Fort Worth force who had helped set off this whole chain reaction of violence.

"Wait a minute!" the detective snapped when he saw Skeeter and Jasper. "Where do you two think you're going?"

"Home," Jasper said, his voice rasping from tiredness.

"Lieutenant Harkness said we could go," Skeeter added.

The detective glowered. "Well, I didn't say you could. Go back up there to those chairs and park it. I may have some more questions in a few minutes."

Jasper protested, "We've already told you everything we know. You got no right to hold us."

One of the vice cops grinned and said, "You'd better shut up before you dig yourself a nice hole, mister. Just do like

Lieutenant Myers says." To the detective, he went on, "Come on, Myers, let's go talk to that captain of yours."

Harkness emerged from his office and came up behind Skeeter and Jasper in time to hear the vice officer's statement. He slipped around the two civilians and frowned. "What's going on?" he asked.

"These men are Officers Brannon and Turner from Fort Worth. They've got some new information on the Hobson case," the detective called Myers said. "We were just going to fill the captain in on it, then we'll want to talk to the suspects again."

"Oh." Harkness grimaced. "I didn't know they *were* suspects."

Myers, a bulky, middle-aged man, just grinned. "Everybody is a suspect, John, you know that."

"Yeah, sure." Harkness turned to Skeeter and Jasper. "Sorry, folks. You'd better do like the lieutenant says."

Skeeter bit back her anger. Harkness looked genuinely regretful as he spoke to them, but she was still leery. Most of her bad temper was directed toward the two vice cops—Brannon and Turner, Myers had called them. They moved past with smug smiles on their faces, and Skeeter couldn't help thinking that she and Jasper were about to get screwed.

As Myers, Brannon, and Turner disappeared into another office, Skeeter turned to Harkness and asked, "Do you know what this is about, Lieutenant?"

He shook his head. "Afraid not. I didn't know anything about it until I came out and saw Lieutenant Myers talking to you. As far as I'm concerned, you're in the clear. But . . . it's not my case. Lieutenant Myers is in charge. I was just helping him out by handling some of the interrogations."

In other words, Skeeter thought, they shouldn't waste their time waiting for any help from him. He and Myers were the same rank, and besides, it was a rare cop who would meddle in what he considered another officer's business.

"Just have a seat," Harkness went on. "I'm sure it won't be much longer."

Skeeter and Jasper traded bleak looks, then sighed and went back up the hall to the short row of metal chairs. As he sat down, Jasper said, "Ever been railroaded, Skeeter?"

"Not yet."

"I was, once. Was down in Mexico, stopped to help a stranger broke down on the side of the road. Never saw the fella before, but he was an American, you know how it is. *Federales* jumped us. Turned out the guy had five hundred pounds of marijuana hidden in various places around his car. The Mexican cops figured me for his partner and the son of a gun let 'em think so. Even told 'em that I planned the whole thing. Cops didn't believe him about that part 'cause they'd been keepin' their eyes on him, but I still wound up doin' two years in their *juzgado*. Lemme tell ya, darlin', even Dallas is better'n a Mexican jail."

"Jasper, I think that's the longest speech I've ever heard you make."

"Yeah, well, I talk when I get nervous. And I don't like the way this is shapin' up, Skeeter."

Neither did she. Fifteen minutes went by, then Myers appeared in the door of the captain's office and said, "You two step in here, please." Despite the polite phrasing, his voice was hard and cold.

Skeeter and Jasper went in and found a man in uniform sitting behind a desk. Brannon and Turner leaned against the wall, arms crossed, wearing their usual Western garb and hats, those arrogant smiles still in place. That was a bad sign, Skeeter thought. The captain was a graying, serious-faced man who looked more like a high school math teacher than a cop. He sounded like a cop, though, as he said, "I understand you two have not been read your rights, is that correct?"

"We haven't been arrested," Skeeter pointed out. "I used to be a lawyer, so I know how they go. We're just trying to cooperate with your investigation, sir."

That drew a thin smile. "And we appreciate that, Ms. Barlow. However, at this point, I'd like for Lieutenant Myers to read you your rights so that we're all sure you understand them."

Skeeter wanted to tell him to put those rights where the sun don't shine, but she pressed her lips together, narrowed her eyes, and reached over to take Jasper's hand. This was looking worse by the second. Jasper squeezed her fingers tightly, and she took a little comfort from that.

By the time Myers had finished the usual Miranda ritual, Skeeter's pulse had settled down to a more normal rate, and she forced a blanket of calm over her feelings. This was all a mistake and nothing that couldn't be worked out in the long run.

"Now," the captain said, "these officers from Fort Worth tell me that you and Frank Hobson were involved together in a gambling operation, is that correct, Ms. Barlow?"

Skeeter stared at him in disbelief for a second, then her gaze snapped over to Brannon and Turner. "You know good and well that's not true!"

"Come on, Ms. Barlow," the one with the mustache said condescendingly. "You've been to Hobson's house several times in the last ten days, you met him at that bar where you work, and you spoke to him at the site of a criminal activity."

"You're talking about the dogfight?"

"What else?" the other one asked.

"Well, that's just crazy. I was at Hobson's house on a case I was working on, and he came into the Horsehead to meet somebody else. It was just an accident that I was there. As for the dogfight . . ." Skeeter took a deep breath. "You boys were there, too."

The one with the mustache smiled. "We were working in our capacity as undercover officers. I hardly think that's your excuse."

"Which one are you?" Skeeter asked.

"I'm Officer Brannon. This is Officer Turner."

"Well, I won't say I'm glad to meet you, 'cause I'm not." She turned to the captain. "This is all a stupid mistake. You can call my boss at the Hallam Agency, Lars Gilford. He'll tell you why I was looking for Frank Hobson. The client would probably be willing to testify about the job I was on, too."

"Who is this client?" the captain asked.

Skeeter hesitated. Now that Hobson was dead, Tracy Roberts didn't have anything to worry about, but it still went against Skeeter's grain to reveal a client's identity. She decided to pass the buck. "Mr. Gilford can tell you that if he deems it proper," she said.

The captain shrugged, but he didn't look particularly pleased by her response. He asked, "What was that about a dogfight?"

Brannon jumped in before Skeeter could answer. "That's a matter of an ongoing investigation involving a task force spread out over several counties, Captain. I'm going to have to ask you to take our word for it without going into all the details. As we told you, it involves illegal dogfights and a great deal of gambling, organized by Frank Hobson and Ms. Barlow here—who, by the way, were involved in a violent altercation with each other earlier tonight at the club where she works."

So the vice cops didn't want her spilling all she knew about the dogfights at the Rising Star Ranch, Skeeter thought. Although Brannon's statement had been directed at the captain, it was for her benefit as much as his. But they were the ones who had brought it up. They were walking a thin line concerning what they did and didn't want revealed. "Except for the fight with Hobson, that's a pack of lies," she said hotly. "Hobson was just a flunky at those dogfights, and I didn't have a thing to do with them!"

Jasper put a hand on her arm. "Take it easy, Skeeter," he advised quietly.

She shook him off. "Easy!" She leveled a finger at Brannon and Turner and said to the captain, "These two yahoos must be in it up to their necks, otherwise they wouldn't be trying to shut me up. They figured you were some stupid cop from the suburbs who'd follow their lead and lock me up for killing Hobson. That way nobody would believe me when I started talking about how they're right in the hip pockets of those gamblers!"

Skeeter saw a flash of something—fear, anger, both?—in the eyes of the two vice cops. It was there just for a fraction of a second and then it was gone, but that was long enough. She was sure she had stumbled on the truth.

Brannon and Turner were as dirty as they could be.

The captain was glaring at her. "Those are very serious charges, Ms. Barlow," he said. "Can you substantiate them in any way?"

She glanced at Brannon and Turner and saw the hatred smoldering in their gazes. "Why don't you call their boss over in Fort Worth? I'll bet there's not even an investigation going on. They made the whole thing up."

"That's ridiculous," Turner snapped. "Sure, go ahead, Captain. Make the call. Ask for Captain Markham in Vice. Hell, call the chief himself."

After a moment, the captain said, "Not at this hour. You men should know that I *will* be checking out your story."

They were still looking indignantly at Skeeter. "Of course," Turner said. "We'd expect you to, Captain."

This still wasn't working out, Skeeter thought desperately. She glanced at Jasper, saw the worried look on his face. He looked over at her and said quietly, "Woo-woo."

"What?" Lieutenant Myers snapped. "What was that, mister?"

"Nothing," Jasper said. "Just clearin' my throat."

The captain glared at him. "If you've got something to say, Mr. Lowe, go ahead and say it."

"No, sir. Sorry."

Skeeter knew all too well what Jasper had meant by that train sound, though.

Railroaded.

The captain frowned in thought for several moments, then said, "I want you to know, Ms. Barlow, that I don't believe for a second these officers are guilty of any wrongdoing, even though as a matter of routine I will confirm what they've told me. However, it seems to me that their accusations against you are a bit premature and lacking in any solid evidence. The investigation into Hobson's death will continue, and I don't want you leaving this area. Do you understand?"

Skeeter nodded gratefully, knowing that she had come within a whisker to being in jail and charged with murder. The worst of it was that she might have taken Jasper along with her.

"The two of you are free to go," the captain said.

Skeeter glanced at Brannon and Turner but couldn't read their expressions. They had probably been hoping she'd be arrested. Being charged with murder would have damaged her credibility severely, would have almost wiped it out, in fact. Any story she had told then would have been dismissed by most people as the grasping at straws of an accused killer. She supposed that Brannon and Turner had accomplished what they had set out to do.

"Come on, Skeeter," Jasper said. "Let's go home."

Chapter Fifteen

She had left her pickup parked on the street near her house, and they had taken Jasper's van to the municipal complex where the police department was located, followed by the cops who had answered the dead body report. Skeeter was still seething as they walked out of the building and headed for the van in the parking lot. She said, "That was nothing but a pack of lies!"

"You know it and I know it," Jasper said. "Don't figure that's goin' to do much good."

Skeeter sighed. "You're right. Brannon and Turner did their damage."

Jasper opened the door for her, then got in and started the van. As he pulled out of the parking lot, he asked, "Do you think those two are on the take?"

Skeeter laughed grimly. "I said it because I was mad at 'em and it was the worst thing I could think of, I guess. But the more I think about it, the more sense it makes. Somehow, they got wind of those dogfights and managed to get into the inner circle. They knew Hobson was part of it, so they probably kept an eye on his place. They saw me there and wanted to know my connection, so they came to the Horsehead and then chased me later on the freeway." She was putting the theory together as she spoke, but it made sense.

"How do you figure they're crooked? They could've done all that as part of their job as undercover officers."

Skeeter shrugged. "Just a hunch. Think about how much money they could make by offering to protect Roy Danby from any investigation."

The streets were practically deserted at this time of the morning, although workers on their way to early jobs would start stirring soon. Jasper said, "Those fellas sicced Hobson on you. Don't seem like honest cops would do such a thing."

"I was just thinking about that," Skeeter agreed.

Drawing a deep breath, Jasper asked, "Now, is there any of this we can *prove?*"

"I don't see how."

Skeeter heard the resignation and defeat in her own voice and didn't like it. Brannon and Turner had boxed her in neatly. Their accusations and innuendoes might not be enough to get her convicted or even charged with murder— not unless they manufactured some more evidence, that is— but what they had done so far would be more than sufficient to put a black cloud over her head for a long time. She might even lose her P.I. license.

Well, Jasper wouldn't fire her from her job as his head of security, she was sure of that. Of course, if word got out that the cops considered him a suspect along with her in Hobson's death, he might lose his liquor license and have to close down the Horsehead.

Might as well face it, she told herself. With a couple of cops like Brannon and Turner lined up on the opposite side, there were all kinds of things they could do to make her life a living hell.

They had almost reached El Campo, the street where Jasper lived, when Skeeter said abruptly, "Shoot, you could have taken me home, Jasper. With Hobson dead, there's no reason to be worried about going back there."

"Nothin' wrong with havin' friends and lettin' 'em take care of you every once in a while, Skeeter."

"Yeah," she said grimly, "except taking care of me got you mixed up in a murder."

Jasper shrugged. "Wasn't your doin'."

Skeeter was glad she had a friend and boss like Jasper.

They turned onto El Campo, and a block and a half later, Jasper angled toward the curb. His headlights washed over a man leaning against the rear fender of a parked car. "Who's that?" Jasper asked.

"Parked in front of your house?"

"Yeah, that's my place, all right. That's one of those cops, isn't it?"

The man was squinting against the headlights as Jasper pulled up, but he didn't lift an arm to shield his face from their glare. Skeeter recognized him as Lieutenant Harkness, the detective who had interrogated her back in White Settlement. What the devil was he doing here at Jasper's house?

Jasper punched the headlight switch and killed the motor. He and Skeeter got out at the same time. Skeeter pushed her door closed, and said, "Hello, Lieutenant. Think of some more questions you want to ask?"

Harkness straightened from his casual pose against the car. "Actually, I did," he replied. "I want to ask you about Brannon and Turner. What makes you think they're dirty?"

Skeeter answered honestly. "I know I didn't kill Hobson, and I don't think Brannon and Turner did either, since they were the ones who sent him after me in the first place. Only thing I can figure out is that they're trying to shut me up about something, and since Hobson didn't do the job for them, they seem to want to take advantage of his death to discredit me."

"Tough, aren't you?"

Jasper said, "Mister, you don't know how tough she can be."

"Maybe I'll find out." Harkness crossed his arms over his

chest. His slender figure didn't look threatening, but Skeeter sensed there was a core of steel there. "I talked to the captain right after you left. Brannon and Turner were already gone; they lit out in a hurry. Lieutenant Myers and the captain have the two of you figured as Hobson's killers, but I don't buy everything Brannon and Turner had to say."

Skeeter returned the level look he was giving her and wished that she could see his features better. She wondered why he was doing this. To gain a little more time, she said, "If you talked to your captain after we left, how'd you beat us here?"

"I didn't expect to. In fact, I went by your house first, Ms. Barlow, and when I didn't find you there, I decided to check the address Mr. Lowe gave us. The two of you must have taken your time getting here."

"Don't speed," Jasper said. "And we were tryin' to hash all this out and decide what to do next."

"And what did you decide?"

Jasper shook his head. "That we were in a hell of lot of trouble."

"Maybe not."

A feeling of impatience nagged at Skeeter. "Just what is it you want from us, Lieutenant?"

"I want you to know that not everybody has you convicted, Ms. Barlow." Harkness shrugged. "This isn't my case, but the department is fairly small. Everybody sort of helps out on most cases. I'm going to be keeping an eye on this one, and if you run across anything, give me a call."

"You figure I'm going to go out and try to solve Hobson's murder? This ain't a TV show, Lieutenant."

"I know that." Harkness's voice was serious now. "But I've always been a little leery of these multi-agency task forces."

"You're willing to admit that Brannon and Turner might be crooked?"

"I'm saying I've got an open mind on the matter." Harkness turned, walked along the side of his car, and opened the door. "Keep in touch, Ms. Barlow."

Skeeter and Jasper didn't say anything as Harkness started his car and drove off, the red taillights winking at them for a couple of blocks and then disappearing in a turn. Finally Jasper said, "Am I mistaken, or did that ol' boy just tell you to look for whoever killed Hobson?"

"That's what he was after, all right," Skeeter said. "He didn't believe Brannon and Turner, but he can't go against them on the record. So he wants me to do the dirty work."

"And save your own rear in the process."

"Reckon there is that to consider," Skeeter said as Jasper led her into the house. And she considered her rear pretty important.

When she woke up, she didn't know where she was or what time it was. Skeeter opened her eyes, pushed herself up on her elbows, and looked around, saw she was lying on a kingsize bed in a room with light blue walls. She sat up. She was wearing a man's pajama top and her panties. After running her fingers through her tangled hair a couple of times, she yawned. The blinds over the room's single window were closed, the curtain pulled shut over them, but she could see sunlight peeping around the edges of the barrier. It was afternoon, she thought.

She stepped out into the hall and heard music coming from her right. Heading in that direction, she came to the bathroom and stopped there first before going on into the kitchen. She found Jasper listening to another radio and cooking an omelet at the stove. The aroma of peppers, onions, bacon, potatoes, and eggs blending together made her realize just how hungry she really was.

"Hope that's for me," she said.

He jumped. "Dammit, Skeeter, don't go sneakin' up on a man like that." He was holding a spatula up in front of him like a weapon.

"I'm sorry, Jasper. Didn't mean to spook you. Do you have any diet Dr. Pepper?"

He pointed with the spatula toward a large white refrigerator. "I've got plain Dr. Pepper, but not diet. Help youself, if you want it," he said. "Glasses're in the cabinet right above."

"Thanks." She nodded to the skillet and said, "If that's for me, put in a few more peppers."

Jasper grinned as he reached for some *jalapenos* on the counter. "You sure you know what you're doin'? I mean, this is breakfast for you."

"Son, you're talking to a lady who thinks there's nothing better in the world for breakfast than cold meatloaf sandwiches."

Jasper shuddered but went back to his cooking.

"I was pretty well out of it when you put me to bed earlier. I do anything I ought to know about?"

"Nope," he said without looking up from the omelet. "Not unless nobody's ever told you that you snore."

"I do not!"

"Well, I didn't tape record it for proof, so you'll have to take my word for it."

Skeeter sat at the table with her glass of Dr. Pepper as he slipped the omelet from the pan onto a plate and got a fork from one of the drawers. He came over to her and placed it in front of her. "We're goin' to have to figure out what to do next."

She picked up the fork, cut off a bite of the omelet, and put

145

it in her mouth. It tasted mild enough at first, but the heat from the peppers grew rapidly and brought moisture to her eyes. Her tastebuds felt almost seared. In a hoarse whisper, she said, "That's good."

"Glad you like it. But what about Hobson?"

Skeeter sighed. "You just won't let a girl eat breakfast in peace, will you?"

"Nope."

"All right, then. It's real simple. I've got to find out who killed him."

It was Jasper's turn to sigh. "I was afraid you were goin' to say that. That's a job for the cops, Skeeter. They're not all crooked."

She looked at him in surprise. "You were the one who was talking about being railroaded."

"Yeah, and I still think we were. But we're not equipped to go out and investigate a killing."

"That's what Harkness wants us to do. Besides, I'm a private detective, remember?"

"Yeah, but not a TV one. Remember? That's what you told Harkness."

She just wished she was looking for the murderer of someone else. Part of her felt like whoever it turned out to be deserved a medal for ridding the world of Hobson.

Jasper sighed. "You're goin' through with this, aren't you?"

"Not much else I can do. But it's not your worry, Jasper."

"The heck it's not! Those White Settlement cops think I'm an accomplice at the very least."

"So I'd think you'd be anxious to find out who shot Hobson."

"Not at the risk of you gettin' hurt!"

Skeeter let her fork clatter onto the plate with the remains of the omelet. She understood now. He didn't want her continuing with the investigation because he was worried about her. He *cared* about her.

"Jasper . . ." she began softly.

"Now don't you go gettin' all mushy on me," he snapped. "I admit, your legs look a whole heck of a lot better stickin' out from under them pajamas than my spindly ol' shanks ever did. But I'm too old for you, for one thing, and for another, you're the best bouncer the Horsehead's ever had. If you and me get sweet on each other, that's liable to foul up everything else."

"So what do we do?"

He didn't say anything for a long moment, then, "I reckon you could go on bein' the best friend I ever had."

Skeeter took a deep breath. "Friends can still fool around."

"Not where I come from."

"All right." Skeeter pushed back her chair and stood up. She started around the table but stopped and put a hand on his shoulder. "Thanks for the omelet, Jasper, and for the bed."

"You're welcome to both. Any time."

Skeeter grinned. "Take you up on it again one of these days."

Then she went to get dressed—and get started looking for a killer.

Jasper had driven her back to her house where she quickly changed clothes, called Rita with an update, and then the cleaning service the agency used. An hour later, dressed in a short, tight denim skirt and a dark brown cotton shirt, Skeeter walked into the offices of the Hallam Agency and drew a grin from Tommy Fuller, who was rummaging in the reception desk. "Hi, Skeeter," he said.

"Hi, yourself." She glanced at the watch on her left wrist. "What are you doing here? Don't you have classes this afternoon?"

"I'm cutting 'em. We didn't know if you'd be in today or not, what with everything that happened last night."

Skeeter nodded wearily. "I guess the cops've been here."

"Oh, yeah. Nearly all morning. They questioned Mr. Gilford and me, but there wasn't much we could tell them except the bare facts of the Roberts case. Speaking of that, I think they were going to call the Brownwood police and get them to check on Mrs. Roberts and her family. I didn't get the impression they considered her a serious suspect in Hobson's murder, however."

"That's no surprise. They've got me figured for it."

"Looks to me like somebody made a clean sweep," Tommy said. "First the dog, then Hobson."

Skeeter nodded. "I've been thinking about that, too. Could be the same person. Whoever killed Raider had a grudge against Hobson. Maybe it built up to the point where revenge wasn't enough and whoever it was wanted him dead."

Tommy started to say something else, but Lars Gilford stuck his head out his office door and beckoned Skeeter. "I thought I heard you out here. I need to talk to you."

Skeeter glanced at Tommy and cocked an eyebrow. Gilford didn't sound happy. The young man shrugged and tried to smile encouragingly. Skeeter went down the hall to Gilford's office.

As she settled herself in the chair she said, "Sorry the cops have been such a nuisance."

Gilford looked across at her, his features carefully controlled. "What with the break-in yesterday morning and the questioning today, I suppose I should be getting used to them. This . . . dog case of yours has caused quite a bit of uproar."

Skeeter shrugged. She'd already apologized once, and she didn't feel like doing it again. "I wasn't trying to do anything except help Tracy Roberts."

"I know that. By the way, how are you feeling? I know you had a rough day yesterday."

Well, a little concern was better than none, Skeeter supposed. She smiled and said, "I've felt better, but I'm all right. I'll be fine once I've found out who killed Hobson."

Gilford's high forehead creased in a frown. "You're going to get involved in an active police investigation? Of a murder?"

"I'm already involved," she pointed out, "right up to my neck, Lars. The cops think I shot Hobson. I've got to prove 'em wrong."

As he leaned back in his chair, Gilford slowly shook his head. After a moment, he said, "I suppose I shouldn't be surprised, knowing you as I do, Skeeter. You're taking all of this very personally, aren't you?"

"Well, wouldn't you?" Even as she asked the question, she thought that no, he probably wouldn't.

"I don't know. I've never been in such an awkward position. I suppose you intend to devote all your time and energy to this matter, then, until it's resolved."

Skeeter was getting tired of this little dance. She stood up and said, "Look, Lars, if you want me to quit, I'll quit."

Gilford motioned her back into her chair. "Take it easy," he said, and for one of the few times in recent memory, Skeeter saw him smile. "You misunderstood. I don't want you to quit. Admittedly, the events of the past few days have caused some problems for the agency, but that's to be expected from time to time. After all, in our line of work we do sometimes have to deal with all sorts of deranged individuals. No, what I was going to suggest is that you go ahead and take the vacation and sick time you have coming, so that you can devote your efforts to finding Hobson's killer without having to worry about your salary or your job."

Skeeter blinked in surprise, unsure what to say. Finally, she managed, "Well, thanks, Lars. That's mighty generous of you—"

"Not at all. This is one of the agency's smaller branches, Skeeter, but also one of its most successful, thanks in large part to you. I've already spoken on the phone this morning to Elizabeth Hallam, and she told me to offer you any help that we possibly can."

"Well, I appreciate that. You sure that you and Tommy can hold down the fort by yourselves?"

"I think we'll manage," Gilford said dryly. "You go ahead and do whatever is necessary, and don't hesitate to call us if you need help." He steepled his fingers in their usual pose. "What are you going to do first?"

"There's plenty of folks besides me who might have wanted Frank Hobson dead," Skeeter said. "Reckon I'll try to find out where they all were last night when somebody blew his brains out."

Chapter Sixteen

Finding Hobson's killer was easier talked about than done, Skeeter knew. She was going to start with the most obvious suspect in any murder—the wife.

Laurie Hobson had a violent temper; Skeeter knew that from her encounter with the woman the day before. Her neighbors had painted Laurie as the sweet, long-suffering type, but she hadn't matched that description when she was trying to stab Skeeter with a sharp comb handle. Skeeter could imagine Laurie putting a .38 against the side of Hobson's head and pulling the trigger.

A dark blue Buick Skylark with an impressive collection of dings and dents was parked in front of the Hobson house. Had to be Laurie's car, Skeeter thought. With her and Frank working overlapping shifts in different directions, she had to have some sort of transportation, too.

Skeeter frowned a little as she parked behind the Buick. When Hobson was in the Horsehead telling her about Raider's death, he had mentioned finding the dog's body when he and Laurie got back to the house after he'd picked her up at work. Why had he been picking her up if Laurie had her own car?

She rapped sharply on the door and waited, more than a little tense. Considering how her last meeting with Laurie Hobson had gone, Skeeter wasn't sure what to expect from her under these circumstances.

The door suddenly swung back a few inches and Laurie Hobson peered at her through the glass of the storm door.

Laurie looked haggard, her hair hanging loosely around her face and her eyes as dull and lifeless as those of a stuffed animal. She didn't seem to recognize Skeeter, because she said, "Yeah? What is it?"

"It's me, Mrs. Hobson, Skeeter Shively." Still no recognition. "I knew your husband." And yesterday you were calling me names and attacking me yourself, she felt like adding.

Laurie's spine stiffened. "Yeah, I remember you now. What the hell do you want?" She didn't ask her visitor to come in.

That was just fine with Skeeter. She said, "I just wanted to tell you how sorry I am about your husband."

"Sorry?"

"Yes, ma'am, I sure am," Skeeter lied.

"I guess it's good somebody is. I'm sure as hell not." Laurie started to shut the door.

"Look, Mrs. Hobson, I'm not what you think I am," Skeeter said quickly. "I barely knew your husband, and I sure wasn't carrying on with him. But I'd like to see whoever killed him get what's coming to him."

Laurie paused. She laughed harshly and said, "You mean a medal?"

There was genuine anger in her voice as Skeeter said, "He was your husband. Most women would want to see justice done."

"Maybe it was. Look, lady, I've got funeral arrangements to make. I don't know what you're really doing here, but I don't have time for you. Just leave me alone."

No point in worrying about offending Laurie's sensibilities, Skeeter realized. She said bluntly, "I figure whoever killed your husband's dog is the same one who shot him. You got any idea who that might have been?"

For the first time, Laurie's eyes lit up, but Skeeter

couldn't tell if it was with fear or anger or both. Abruptly, Laurie pushed open the storm door and came out onto the porch, making Skeeter step back hurriedly.

"Who the hell do you think you are, Nancy Drew?"

Time to back off a little. "No ma'am," Skeeter said. "I'm just worried. I was involved with some of the same people your husband was involved with."

"You think one of those rich people from the dogfights killed Frank?" Laurie blinked solemnly, as if the idea hadn't occurred to her until now. Then she shook her head. "No, I don't think so. Frank wasn't important enough for any of them to dirty their hands on. Except for one of those stupid bimbos who *liked* the fact that he was a grubby little nobody. She liked the idea that she was screwing a common man." With a sneer, Laurie went on, "She didn't know that they don't come any more common than Frank Hobson."

Laurie was talking about Martina Danby, Skeeter realized. From the sound of it, though, Laurie didn't know which of the women who patronized the dogfights at the Rising Star Ranch her husband had been sleeping with.

"Well, I'm thinking twice about having any business dealings with those people," she said. "Even if I could make some money by selling dogs to them." Skeeter shook her head. "Sure was a shame about Raider."

"Yeah, well, I don't miss him. He was the only thing I ever saw with a worse disposition than Frank. I begged him and begged him to get rid of that dog, but he just laughed in my face. Said I'd go before the dog would." Laurie crossed her arms over her chest and smiled thinly. "I guess he found out different."

Now that Laurie had calmed down a little and seemed more willing to talk, Skeeter decided to push a little harder. "I guess the police have been out here a lot."

"Not really. A Wise County deputy came in the middle of the night and told me Frank had been killed. He took me down to Fort Worth to identify the body. Then he took me over to the police station down there in White Settlement. The cops there asked me a lot of questions." Her lips were still curved in that sardonic smile. "They wanted to know if I had an alibi. I was surprised they weren't more interested when I told them I was by myself all night."

That was because the cops already had a suspect, Skeeter thought—her.

"I guess they figured you couldn't've killed your own husband."

"Well, that's jumping to a conclusion, isn't it?" Laurie stopped smiling and glared at Skeeter. "Look, like I said, I've got funeral arrangements to make. Do whatever you want about Frank's buddies and those dogfights. Just go away and don't bother me again, okay?"

Skeeter shrugged. "Sure. Thanks for hearing me out."

"Yeah, yeah." Laurie opened the storm door, stepped inside, let it slam behind her, then shoved the wooden door firmly closed.

That was one unpleasant woman, Skeeter thought as she got back into the pickup. But that didn't make her a killer. There were plenty of unpleasant people in the world who never really hurt anybody. Skeeter drove away from the house and glanced up at the gray sky overhead. Twilight would come early today, but there was still plenty of time to drive to Decatur. She wanted to find out a little more about Laurie Hobson.

She found a parking place a few doors down from the beauty shop near the square. The place was doing more business today. All three chairs were occupied, and only two operators were on duty: a thick-bodied woman in her fifties with short white hair, and a young woman around twenty with long blonde hair. The older woman was working back and forth between two of the customers while the blonde handled the third one. As Skeeter came in, the older woman glanced up and said, "I'm sorry, honey. We won't be able to work you in today."

Skeeter smiled. "Oh, that's all right. I was just looking for a friend of mine. Laurie Hobson? She still works here, doesn't she?"

Five heads turned and looked at her in surprise.

Skeeter frowned slightly and asked, "What's wrong?"

"Oh, dear," the older woman said. "You haven't heard?"

"Heard what?"

The blonde said, "Laurie's husband was killed last night."

Skeeter let her eyes widen in shock. "Killed? Oh, my Lord, poor Laurie. What happened? Was it a car wreck?"

Scissors still poised over the hair of the woman in her chair, the blonde leaned toward Skeeter and said in a conspiratorial tone, "He was murdered!"

"Ginger!" the older woman snapped. "Beauty shops have enough of a reputation for gossip. Don't add to it, dear."

"Sorry, Mrs. Harris," the blonde muttered, turning her attention back to the customer in her chair.

Skeeter stood there with that stunned look still on her face for a moment, then said, "Do you mind if I sit down for a minute?"

"Not at all," Mrs. Harris said. "Please, have a seat."

"The news just threw me a little. Poor Laurie." Skeeter sank down on one of the chairs in the waiting area.

"We're all very upset about it," Mrs. Harris said. "Laurie hadn't been working here for very long, but we were all fond of her."

Then you must not know her very well, Skeeter thought. She kept that to herself. "She and I are old friends. I worked with her at the Fashion Ranch in Fort Worth."

Mrs. Harris smiled. "You're not looking for a job, are you? As you can see, we're short-handed. We will be until Laurie comes back to work."

"No, I just wanted to come by and say hi to her," Skeeter replied with a shake of her head. "Did the police catch the man who did it?"

The blonde started to say something again, but a sharp glance from Mrs. Harris sent her back to her work. The older woman said, "I'm afraid not. It could've been almost anybody, you know. Fort Worth is such a dangerous place. All sorts of dope addicts, drug dealers, and gangs down there. It's just not safe there anymore. Why, I remember when you could go to Fort Worth and ride the bus from Leonard's parking lot into downtown, and it was so nice. I used to go shopping at Leonard's and Stripling's and Cox's and The Fair . . ."

Skeeter was prepared to sit there and listen to Mrs. Harris reminisce for an hour if need be, if it would help her figure out who had killed Hobson. But the white-haired woman shook her head abruptly.

"You don't want to listen to an old lady's memories," she said. "Not when you've just heard such disturbing news. Did you know Laurie's husband well, too?"

Skeeter shook her head. "Not really. I saw him a few times when he came to pick her up from work. Did he come by here every day to get her like he did when they lived down there?"

"Oh, no, she has her own car." Mrs. Harris frowned, a hint of suspicion appearing in her eyes for the first time. "I thought Laurie'd had that car for a while. Didn't she have it while they were in Fort Worth?"

"Sure she did. But it was in the shop a lot."

Mrs. Harris shrugged. "Oh." She was noticeably cooler in her attitude now, as if she had decided that Skeeter was just prying in something that was none of her business. The woman evidently had an aversion to gossip, probably because she was surrounded by it all day in the beauty shop.

The blonde, Ginger, spoke up again, braving Mrs. Harris's displeasure. "That car of Laurie's does break down some," she said. "Why, I had to loan her my car to run an errand last Saturday. No, wait a minute, it was the Saturday before that."

Mrs. Harris turned toward her. "Nobody told me about that."

Ginger looked distinctly uncomfortable, but she had already gotten herself into this. "It wasn't busy," she said quickly. "We had a customer under the dryer and I was washing another lady's hair, but that was all that was going on. Laurie said it would only take a half-hour or so, and she was right. She was back in about thirty-five minutes. No harm done."

"Hmmph," Mrs. Harris said, going back to the two customers she had been working on.

Ginger looked past her at Skeeter. "Laurie said her water pump kept going out." The young blonde frowned. "Come to think of it, her husband picked her up that evening."

Skeeter thought back. The day Ginger was talking about was the same day Raider had wound up dead, his throat slashed. Skeeter had eliminated Laurie Hobson as a suspect because she'd thought that Laurie was with her husband during the time the dog was killed. Now that no longer seemed to be the case. That half-hour errand could have been driving the borrowed car to and from Boyd. The time frame allowed a few minutes for cutting Raider's throat. And the dog had probably been accustomed enough to having her around that she could have gotten close to him. A quick thrust and jerk with a sharp knife, and Raider wouldn't have had time to fight back. Such a task would require a clear head and icy nerves; if the job was bungled, the victim might still bleed to death, but in Raider's case, the dog would have had time before dying to rip Laurie to pieces.

A woman who could do something like that probably wouldn't flinch at shooting a much-hated husband.

Skeeter took a deep breath. She was getting ahead of herself. What she'd found out here at the beauty shop was interesting, but it didn't prove anything.

"I've got to be going," she said.

"Are you going by to see Laurie?" Mrs. Harris asked.

"No, ma'am, I've got to head back to Fort Worth," Skeeter said.

"Better you than me," Mrs. Harris said fervently. "Fort Worth is full of crime."

"Yes, ma'am," Skeeter nodded as she was leaving. "It sure is."

Chapter Seventeen

Even though what she'd learned at the beauty shop pointed to Laurie Hobson as Raider's killer, Skeeter knew she couldn't afford to jump to any conclusions. Just because Laurie might have cut the dog's throat didn't mean she'd shot her husband. There were other people who might have wanted Frank Hobson dead, like his business partner and his mistress—who just happened to be married to each other.

She drove on toward Denton, slowing when she saw the gate of the Rising Star Ranch up ahead. It was open, and there was no guard in sight today. No black ribbon tied on the oak tree, either. Skeeter took the turn and headed toward the ranch headquarters on the narrow road.

Skeeter parked her pickup in front of the house. A gate of black wrought-iron was open at the moment, and the walk went through it onto a flagstone patio. A massive wooden door with an ornate brass knocker in the center of it was on the other side of the patio. Skeeter walked across the flagstones and started to reach for the knocker, but the door opened before she could touch it.

Roy Danby had a welcoming smile on his face, but his eyes were filled with cool suspicion as he said, "Skeeter! What brings you out here into the boonies?"

"I'm surprised you remember me, Mr. Danby," Skeeter said, ignoring his question for the moment.

"Never forget a pretty woman or a good dog, that's my rule. Come in."

He stepped back and ushered Skeeter into the house.

"Come on into the living room," Danby said. "Martina and I were just about to have a drink. Why don't you join us?"

"Thanks," Skeeter said. "Don't mind if I do."

Danby led the way into a large, sprawling living room with a beamed ceiling. A massive fireplace with a mantel of native stone dominated the far side of the room. Above the mantel were hung a set of longhorns flanked by a couple of classic Winchester repeaters, the "Yellow Boy" model. If they were originals, they'd be worth ten to fifteen thousand dollars each, Skeeter knew. Danby had to be doing all right if he could afford to hang twenty to thirty thousand dollars' worth of guns on the wall, she thought. And they were hardly the only weapons in sight. The other walls of the room were decorated with a wide variety of rifles, pistols, and muskets. She even saw a few cavalry sabers and Bowie knives. The place was a veritable museum.

In the center of the room was a colorful Navajo rug. It was surrounded by a pair of long white leather sofas and several overstuffed armchairs of the same material. Martina Danby looked just as sleek and expensive as anything else in the room as she lounged on one of the sofas, a drink in her hand. "Hello, Skeeter," Martina said. "I didn't expect to see you again so soon."

Skeeter thought for a second that Martina was referring to their meeting the day before at Frank Hobson's house, but then she realized the other woman meant their brief introduction on Sunday before the dogfight, a little over forty-eight hours earlier. God, had it only been that long? Skeeter thought.

Roy Danby gestured toward the bar. "What can I get you?"

Skeeter considered, then said, "Well, I was going to say rum and Coke, but since I've got to drive back, you'd better make it just Coke."

"Comin' up," Danby said. He reached under the bar for ice and a glass, then took a canned Coke out of a small refrigerator and poured it. As he carried it over to Skeeter, his expression became more solemn and he said, "I hope you didn't come up here looking for Frank Hobson. If you did, I'm afraid I've got some bad news for you."

She took the drink from him and said, "Thanks . . . No, I know about Frank already. Horrible thing."

"It certainly is. I hope the police catch whoever did it, soon." Danby went back to the bar and poured himself a Scotch. "Were you and Frank good friends?"

Skeeter sipped the Coke and then shook her head. "Not really. I had only met him recently. We had a common interest in dogs, that's all."

"Oh. I thought you and him might've been, well, an item." Danby grinned. "Frank always had an eye for a pretty girl."

Martina lifted her glass to her lips and regarded Skeeter coolly over the rim. Neither woman's face revealed what they really knew about Frank Hobson and his taste in women.

Danby carried his drink over to the sofa and sat down beside his wife. "Please, have a seat," he said, waving to the armchairs. "What can we do for you?"

"Actually, I was hoping you might be able to help me with something."

"Of course," Martina said. "If there's anything we can do . . ."

"Frank said something about knowing people who might be interested in buying dogs from me. I'm just getting started in the breeding business, you see. I don't know if Frank was referring to you two, or to some of your other friends."

Danby nodded. "I understand. As it happens, I'm not in the market for any more dogs, but I do know some people who might be interested. They're going to be out here tomorrow night for a little social occasion, if you'd like to come up and meet them. There's a man named Loomis who might be especially interested in talking to you."

"That would be great," Skeeter said trying not to show the surprise she felt. "I'd really appreciate the introductions."

"Fine, can you be here about seven-thirty?"

"No problem." No problem if Crispin Loomis didn't reveal that her name was really Barlow instead of Shively, she added silently.

Martina gave her a slightly condescending smile. "We'd ask you to stay for dinner, Skeeter, but Roy and I are going out . . ."

Skeeter sipped the Coke again, then stood up. "Oh, no, you've done more than enough for me already. I appreciate the kindness you've shown me. Seven-thirty tomorrow night."

Danby got to his feet. "That's right. Here, I'll show you out."

Skeeter hesitated as he started across the rug toward her. "There's one other thing I was wondering about."

"What's that?"

"Well, this is sort of embarrassing. The police came to see me. You know, about Frank's murder. I guess they found my name and number somewhere among his things and they asked questions."

Danby frowned slightly, and Martina's cool facade seemed a bit shaken, too. "What did you tell them?" Danby asked.

"Oh, don't worry, I didn't say anything about the dogs. I just told them that Frank and I were acquaintances, that we'd met in a bar." Skeeter laughed a little. "I made it sound like Frank tried to pick me up."

Danby looked somewhat reassured. "He would have, if

he'd really met you that way."

"Anyway, they asked me for an alibi, and I was a little worried because I didn't really have one. What I was wondering . . . did they come to see you, too?"

Martina said, "As a matter of fact, they did. I think they were questioning everyone they could find who knew Frank. So I don't think you need to worry about being singled out, dear."

"You mean they asked you two for alibis and everything?"

Danby nodded. "We just told them the truth—I was out with some friends of mine, and Martina spent a quiet evening at home. I don't think you need to worry, Skeeter. It's all just routine." He chuckled and added, "I don't think the cops would ever accuse you of shooting Frank."

"I'm glad to hear that," Skeeter said fervently. "It's really worrisome to get mixed up in something like that."

"Of course," Danby said. "Now, if you'll excuse us . . ."

"Sure. Thanks again."

"You're quite welcome," Martina told her as Danby steered her back toward the entrance foyer.

He waved as she drove off in her pickup.

As the pickup followed the twisting road back toward the highway, she went over what she'd learned. It wasn't a lot, but it might turn out to be important. The main thing was that neither Danby nor Martina had a solid alibi for the night before. Danby's friends would probably be willing to lie for him. Either one of them, Skeeter thought, could have killed Hobson.

Suddenly, she frowned. How would either of the Danbys have known to look for Hobson in front of her house? As far as they knew, she was Skeeter Shively, pit bull breeder, not Skeeter Barlow, private detective. The same was true of

Laurie Hobson. Skeeter let out a moan as she reached for the dashboard and flicked on the headlights. She hadn't thought of that before. Laurie, Danby, and Martina still had to be regarded as suspects in the murder, but they didn't look nearly as likely as they had earlier.

But that still left Loomis.

Her mind was full of questions and half-formed plans, and at first she didn't pay any attention to the headlights that came up behind her. She was vaguely aware of them, but that was all. Suddenly, some warning instinct made her look more intently into the rearview mirror, and she felt a flash of *déjà vu*. The other vehicle had closed up the gap between them and was right on her tail.

"Damn!" Somebody was chasing her again.

Skeeter's foot pressed down heavily on the gas pedal, sending the pickup surging forward. The red needle on the speedometer began to climb steadily. The vehicle behind her increased its speed, too. Skeeter bit back another curse and concentrated on her driving.

Skeeter's heart was thumping wildly. She hated this, hated being chased, like when Brannon and Turner had gotten on her tail on the way home from work that night a week or so earlier.

Suddenly, a red light began to flash on the roof of the pursuing vehicle. Skeeter winced when she first saw the garish pulses in her rearview mirror, then she grimaced and took her foot off the accelerator. She'd panicked, she realized now, and run when there was no reason to. The glare of the following car's headlights had prevented her from noticing that it was a police vehicle of some kind. Skeeter sighed. All her edginess had done was get her a ticket for speeding.

As the pickup slowed, she steered it onto the shoulder, touching the brakes lightly to bring its speed down even more. The other car didn't fall in behind her, as she had expected it to, but stayed on the asphalt of the highway instead. Skeeter frowned in confusion.

Without any warning, the car's motor roared, and it lunged forward until it was beside her. She saw its front fender coming toward the pickup and jerked the wheel to the right, but she was too late. With a bone-jarring impact, car and pickup came together.

The steering wheel was wrenched out of Skeeter's hands by the collision. Her pickup was forced across to the far edge of the shoulder, and the right front tire suddenly dropped onto the embankment that sloped down a few feet from the highway. The left front wheel slid off the shoulder, too, and she suddenly found herself bouncing down the embankment in the pickup. A pasture fence loomed up in front of her. Skeeter jammed on the brakes, but the front end of her vehicle snapped off a fence post. Wires broke with a twanging sound loud enough to be heard even in the cab of the plunging pickup. Finally, after a handful of seconds that seemed like an hour, the pickup came to a shuddering stop some fifty yards into a weed-grown pasture. Somehow, Skeeter found the ignition key and turned it, killing the motor in case of a gasoline leak.

The car that had run her off the road had come to a stop on the shoulder of the highway. Now, as she got out of the pickup and stood on shaky legs and looked in that direction, she could see by the reflected glare of its headlights and the flashing light on its roof that it wasn't an official police car at all. It was an undercover vehicle, and the flasher was one of the portable ones used by off-duty cops and fireman and the like, that attached magnetically to the roof. Two men had left the car, scurried down the embankment, and were running toward her.

Skeeter knew who they were before they ever reached her.

"Miz Barlow, you ought to be more careful," Officer Brannon said as he came trotting up to her. "You could hurt somebody, driving that way."

"Yeah," Officer Turner agreed. "It's a good thing we came along to stop you."

Skeeter clenched her fists as she said, "What do you two want?"

"Just doin' our duty as law officers," Brannon said smugly, "apprehending an unsafe driver."

"Gotta keep our highways safe," Turner added.

Skeeter took a deep breath. "Why don't you tell me what you really want? I know you've either been following me, or you were keeping an eye on Danby's place. Either way you're up to no good." Skeeter thought she sounded remarkably composed considering.

"All right," Brannon said, his voice cold and hard now. "You're poking around in things that don't concern you—"

"The hell they don't! I'm a suspect in Hobson's murder, remember? You're the ones who saw to it that it played that way."

Turner said, "Don't be stupid. You know there's not enough evidence to convict you. You probably won't even be charged."

"But the cops won't ever trust me," Skeeter shot back. "That's what you were after, wasn't it? You didn't want anybody to believe me if I started talking about some of the things I've run across."

"What things would those be?" Brannon asked coolly.

"How about illegal dogfights and high-stakes betting and a pair of cops who're planning to blackmail the very people they're supposed to be busting?"

Even in the dim light of the shadowy field, Skeeter could

see Turner reach toward the small of his back as he let out a curse. For a terrifying moment, she thought she'd pushed him too far. But before Turner could pull his gun, Brannon caught his arm and said sharply, "Hold it! She's just running her mouth."

"But—"

"She can't prove a thing," Brannon said firmly. "Besides, even if she starts spreading stories, she's a suspect in a murder. Like she said, who's going to believe her?" He turned his attention back to Skeeter. "Besides, you've got too much sense to do that, don't you, Barlow? You know if you start going around and spouting a bunch of lies, we'd have no choice but to bring out all of your unsavory background to show what kind of person you really are."

"Unsavory background?" Skeeter echoed. "What are you talking about?"

"Well, let's face it, you work in a honkytonk. And how many men have you slept with in the past year?"

"That's none of your—"

"Oh, but it is my business—if you're accusing me of something illegal. You're a slut, Barlow, and we'll make sure everybody knows it. Including your kids and your ex-husband. Hell, we might even find somebody whose testimony could get you a prostitution charge. And what about drugs? Could be you and that cowboy boss of yours have been dealing out of his club."

"In other words you'd frame me," Skeeter snapped.

Brannon shrugged. "Hey, you use the weapons that are available to you. It's better than a bullet in the head, like you gave Hobson."

"You know I didn't kill him," she said quietly. "Both of you, just leave me alone."

"You going to remember what we told you?"

Her voice was little more than a whisper as she said, "I'll remember."

"Good. You be careful now, you hear?"

Skeeter didn't say anything as she watched them plod out of the field and up the embankment to their car. Several other vehicles had stopped, drawn by the flashing light and the possibility of a nice bloody wreck, but the two officers sent the bystanders on their way. Then they got in their car and drove off. Skeeter kept an eye on their taillights until they vanished.

A wave of dizziness hit her. She put a hand on the crumpled fender of her truck to steady herself, then looked off in the direction where Brannon and Turner had gone.

"Yeah, I'll remember," she whispered, hate in her voice. "I'll remember real good."

Chapter Eighteen

The pickup started the first time she cranked it, and she was grateful for that. She turned it around and drove carefully across the field, through the break in the fence, and up the embankment. Both headlights still worked and thankfully so did the radio. She turned it on and got a nice, smooth, easy ballad. Just the thing for jangled nerves, she thought.

Or it would have been if she'd been able to concentrate on it. She kept thinking about Brannon and Turner instead. Maybe they *had* killed Hobson.

She stopped at the first house she came to, looking for the owner of the fence she had ruined. Luckily, the middle-aged couple who lived there also owned the pasture. They were more concerned that Skeeter was all right, and she assured them she was. Physically, that was true. Her nerves were pretty frazzled.

The rest of the drive to Fort Worth was uneventful, and as Skeeter saw the lights of the city spreading out from one horizon to the other, she took a deep breath and realized that her shakiness was gone. It had been replaced by anger and a deep determination to see this business through to the end.

She pulled into the parking lot of the Horsehead and had no trouble finding a place for the pickup. She glanced at the fender as she got out, then sighed and shook her head at the damage. Sooner or later, somehow, those two yahoos would pay for what they had done, she vowed.

Skeeter went into the club, pausing just inside the doorway to look around. Jasper and Chuckie were behind the

169

bar, doling out drinks to a dozen customers perched on the stools. Spotting her by the door, Jasper nodded and raised a hand in a brief wave of greeting. Even across the room, Skeeter could see the look of concern on his face. She should have called him earlier, she thought, but things had been busy.

As she started toward the bar, one of the drinkers turned around and grinned at her. Buck had a bruise on his face from the run-in with Hobson the night before, but it didn't seem to be bothering him. He lifted his mug of beer and patted the empty stool next to him. Skeeter sidled up and settled her rear end on it.

"Howdy," Buck said. "How you doin', Skeeter?"

"I've been better," she admitted. As Jasper came along the bar and stopped in front of her, she looked up at him and said, "Hi."

"Hi yourself. You ever hear of an invention called the telephone, Skeeter?"

Her temper flared. "I've had things to do. You ought to know that better'n anybody."

Jasper held up his hands in surrender. "Yeah, I know. I was just worried."

"We all were," Buck added.

"Well, I'm sorry if y'all were worried."

"Forget it. You find out anything?"

Skeeter leaned forward. "Maybe. Why don't you get me an iced tea and I'll tell you what happened? You've got to promise you won't get mad and go chargin' off like a bull, though."

"That bad?" Jasper poured the tea and slid it over to her. "I reckon this means you ain't workin' tonight."

She sipped and shook her head. "Sorry, Jasper. I've got to look up Harkness and talk to him."

"Shoot, I can help you with that. Look over your right shoulder."

Skeeter frowned, then turned and peered over her shoulder as he had said. She saw Harkness sitting in one of the booths along the far wall, nursing a beer. She turned back to Jasper and asked, "What's he doing in here?"

"Lookin' for you, I imagine. He sure didn't come to make me rich by drinkin' up all my beer. He's been here an hour, and that's only his second one. And you'll notice it's almost full."

"Guess I'd better go talk to him."

Buck protested, "Wait a minute. You said you were going to tell us what happened to you today."

"Sorry, darlin'. I'll be back in a few minutes." Skeeter picked up her glass and headed for the booth where Harkness sat.

As she slid onto the naugahyde seat across from him, he said, "Hello, Ms. Barlow. I was hoping I'd run into you here."

"Make it Skeeter." She nodded toward his mug of beer. "From the looks of that, I reckon you must be off duty."

He sipped the brew, then said, "You're right, but you know how some cops are. We never really go off duty."

"In other words, you're here to ask me what I've found out about Hobson's murder." Skeeter didn't bother making it a question.

Harkness answered anyway. "That's right. And I might have a few things to tell you, too."

"Such as?"

He shook his head. "Sorry. Ladies first."

Skeeter swallowed her exasperation. "All right," she said. "I've got to backtrack a little first. Back to that dog of Hobson's."

"The one that was killed?"

"Yeah. The first murder in this case. Looks to me like Laurie Hobson is the one who did it."

"I thought you said she was with her husband."

"Mistaken assumption on my part." Quickly, Skeeter told him what she had found out at the beauty shop in Decatur, concluding by saying, "Laurie had a reason all along to kill that dog, and now it looks like she had a chance to do it without Hobson suspecting her."

Harkness nodded slowly. "If she knew her husband wasn't going to be home that day when she borrowed the car from the other girl . . . Yeah, it makes sense. She probably could've gotten close enough to the dog to do it easier than most people. To use the classical terms, means, motive, and opportunity all line up for her."

"That's what I thought."

"But that doesn't mean she killed her husband, too," Harkness pointed out.

"I know it," Skeeter said.

"For one thing, if she did, how'd she know where to find him? She didn't know your real name or where you live, did she?"

Skeeter shook her head. "That whole business has been bothering me. If Hobson had been killed somewhere else, this mess might be easier to figure out. But none of the people involved know who I am—except Crispin Loomis. He knew my real name, and it wouldn't have been hard for him to find my address. He knew that Hobson had it in for me. He might've figured that by staking out my place, he'd come up with Hobson sooner or later."

Harkness leaned back against the seat on his side of the booth and frowned. "This Loomis seems to've gone to ground. We haven't been able to turn up anything on him yet.

He's not at his house in Dallas and not at any of the places he frequents over here. He would be the most logical suspect—if you hadn't turned up on the scene with the same kind of gun as the one that killed Hobson."

With a grimace, Skeeter asked, "Y'all ever find that bullet?"

"That's one of the things I was going to tell you. We did finally locate the bullet. Because your front yard slopes up a little, the bullet's path took it into one of the foundation blocks of your house. Flattened and distorted it enough so that ballistics tests wouldn't tell us anything, but we were able to determine that it came from a .38."

Skeeter felt like groaning. "One more nail in the coffin as far as that fella Myers is concerned, I reckon."

"Myers is convinced of your guilt," Harkness said with a shrug.

"But you're not." This time it was almost a question.

Harkness took a deep breath. "No, I'm not. I did a little checking on you, Ms. Barlow . . . Skeeter. Top of your class in law school, very promising career with a prominent Houston law firm, wealthy family . . . Even if you did chuck all that to become a P.I., I still think you're too smart to have done something like this. If you wanted Hobson dead, you'd go about it smarter."

"Thanks . . . I think." Skeeter paused, then said, "Anyway, you make it sound like I did something dumb by becoming a private detective. I happen to like the work."

"And what about this place?" Harkness waved a hand at their surroundings.

"The Horsehead? I like it, too. I like the people and I like the music. No crime in that, is there?"

"Just wondering how you got here. Growing up, you must've been exposed to the opera and the ballet a lot more than you were to Hank Williams and Willie Nelson."

Skeeter grimaced again. His prying had nothing to do with the case, but it would be easier to tell him what he wanted to know than to stall. "The firm I worked for had as a client a corporation that owned several bars. Another company sued 'em for some sort of trademark infringement, and of course, we got the job of defending them. I was a real go-getter then, a young associate attorney, so I decided to visit some of the plaintiff's bars just to see what sort of ammunition they had. Got me some cowboy duds and went honkytonkin'." She shrugged. "What can I say? I found out I liked it. I was already starting to feel a little penned-in, working in corporate law that way, so when I got the chance, I left. I knew one of the operatives for the Hallam Agency's office in Houston, and he said they needed somebody up here, so here I am." Skeeter grinned.

Harkness had listened to her story in silence. When she was finished, he asked, "What happened with that lawsuit?"

"They settled out of court, of course. I don't know the details. But three years later, all the cowboy stuff was gone and they were bringing in a bunch of ferns and going for the yuppie crowd. I imagine they sued each other over *that,* too."

Harkness chuckled and drained the rest of his beer.

Skeeter turned serious. "What about Brannon and Turner?"

With a frown, Harkness asked, "What about them?"

"They tried to kill me tonight."

The lieutenant's eyes widened in surprise as he stared across the table at her. "Tried to kill you? Are you sure of that?"

"Well, maybe they were just trying to scare me, but they admitted they wouldn't have minded if I'd wound up dead." She told him about being run off the road by the two undercover officers, then said, "Look, Lieutenant, it's got to be obvious what they're up to, even to another cop."

"What do you mean by that?" Harkness asked tightly.

"I mean you don't want to think that a couple of fellow officers are crooks and maybe killers," Skeeter said. "I understand that. But I'm not making any of this up."

Harkness waited a moment, then said, "They really are who they say they are, you know. I heard the captain talking to their boss in Fort Worth. They're on loan to an anti-gambling task force that's working primarily undercover."

"That doesn't surprise me. They're using their position to gather evidence against Roy Danby and the other people who come to bet on those dogfights at Danby's ranch."

"So? That's what they're supposed to be doing."

"Yeah, but if they're straight, why haven't they turned over the evidence they've already got to their bosses? Why haven't Danby and the others been arrested?"

Harkness toyed with his empty mug as he thought. "Maybe Brannon and Turner *have* turned over their evidence. Maybe the bust just hasn't been set up yet."

Skeeter shook her head. "I reckon that's possible, but if that was the case, why are they after me? Why'd they try to shut me up by siccing Hobson on me? And since Hobson wound up dead, they've been doing their best to discredit anything I've got to say."

"They just don't want you interfering—"

"That's right. They don't want me messing up their blackmail scheme. They're about ready to hit Danby up for a payoff, and they want to keep me busy enough I can't stop them."

"But you can't prove any of that. It's your word against theirs."

"I can't prove it . . . yet." An idea had been flitting around in the back of Skeeter's mind, and she decided to plunge ahead and see how Harkness would react to it. "I think I can prove everything I've told you—if you'll help me."

The creases in the lieutenant's forehead deepened. "I'm not sure—"

"I'm talking about proving that Brannon and Turner are dirty. Roy and Martina Danby are having a little get-together at their house tomorrow night for some of their dogfighting friends. I'm willing to bet that Brannon and Turner are going to be there."

"And if they are?"

"They're not going to like it when they see me show up. They'll probably try to warn me off again, and if they do, the conversation is liable to get pretty interesting."

From the look in his eyes, she thought Harkness knew where she was going, but he said, "That'd still be your word against theirs."

"Not if you heard it, too."

"You're talking about wearing a wire."

"That's exactly what I'm talking about."

Harkness sighed heavily. "I can't do that. We haven't got the equipment. White Settlement has a small department compared to Dallas or Fort Worth—"

"The agency has the equipment," Skeeter cut in.

For a long moment, Harkness didn't reply. Finally, he looked across the table at her and said, "This is pretty irregular. Even if it works and you're right, I'll make some enemies. Cops don't like it when one of their own starts spying on his fellow officers. If it doesn't work, I'll be royally screwed."

"Yeah, but if it does work, you'll be catching a couple of crooked cops who might even be murderers."

Harkness tipped his head to one side. "There is that."

"Then you'll do it?"

"I'll think about it. I need some more details first about how the whole thing is going to work."

"You want details?" Skeeter asked with a grin. "I got details."

Chapter Nineteen

"This shouldn't be too hard," Buck Ngyuen said, tapping keys on the keyboard in front of him. "Of course, it may take a while to find the right bank. I could probably go to jail for this, you know."

"I know," Skeeter said. "And I appreciate the help, Buck."

"Shucks, ma'am—"

"Buck, if you say that again, I am going to hit you."

He grinned and kept working on the computer.

Skeeter might not have recognized him if she had seen him on the street. He was wearing a dark suit, a white shirt, and a muted blue tie. His long, slender fingers seemed to move with minds of their own on the keyboard.

It was just after noon on Wednesday, and the two of them were in Buck's apartment. The night before, when Skeeter had broached the subject of breaking into Roy Danby's bank accounts, Buck had agreed immediately, but only on the condition that the computer consulting firm for which he worked not be involved. That had been fine with Skeeter, and they had agreed to meet at his apartment while he was on his lunch hour.

Not surprisingly, the place was full of cowboy paraphernalia—hats, lassos, spurs, chaps. The walls were covered with B-Western movie posters. In one special place of honor were hung two black-and-white eight-by-ten photos, each of them autographed. On the left was Roy Rogers, beside him William Boyd.

"Roy and Hoppy," Buck had said when he saw her looking

at the photos. "My heroes. Pretty strange in this day and age, I guess."

"A fella could do worse for heroes," Skeeter murmured.

They had gotten started right away, and at first Buck had tried to explain to her what he was doing. Skeeter had listened to him for a few minutes, then interrupted, "You might as well be pointing your finger at the screen and saying *Shazam!* for all I know what you're talking about. I know how to turn on the system in the office, type up a file, save it, possibly print it, and turn the blamed thing off. That's all."

"But this is fairly simple—"

"Not to somebody who was born when folks still had black-and-white TV sets. Just do it."

He had shrugged. "Sure." Skeeter hoped she hadn't hurt his little technologically advanced feelings.

"As long as we're just scanning the records and not trying to tamper with them, there's a very slight risk of anybody noticing we're there," Buck said. "Banks have gotten more and more security-conscious when it comes to their computers, but there are still ratholes. They're just too small to carry out any money."

"You're not having any trouble getting into those files," Skeeter commented.

"Yeah, well, my company's set up several security programs, some of them for these very banks. What I'm doing is really a breach of professional ethics."

"I'm sorry, Buck. I shouldn't have asked you to do this."

"Hey, I'm not complaining!" Buck looked over at her and grinned. "Don't you gumshoes have some sort of tradition about playing fast and loose with the rules? You know how the shamus always bends the law a little to see justice done."

"Gumshoes? Shamuses? Let me guess. When you weren't

watching cowboy movies as a kid, you were watching private eye movies."

"I've seen *The Maltese Falcon* thirty-five times."

"Lord help us."

They were prepared for this to take all afternoon if necessary. Skeeter had spent the morning running errands. With the help of Lars Gilford, she had gotten all the apparatus she would need for later, and she wasn't supposed to meet Harkness until five o'clock. Buck had laid the groundwork at his job by saying that he didn't feel well, and he would call in sick for the rest of the day if need be. Skeeter had a feeling that would be the case regardless of how fast they accomplished what they were trying to do. Buck wanted to be in on the wrap-up, as he called it.

She sat on a chair to one side of Buck's computer workstation and watched as he shifted from bank to bank, adroitly getting around the various locks and passwords. Skeeter kept her eyes open for Danby's name. Of course, it was always possible Danby had all his accounts under some corporate name other than the Rising Star Ranch, so she watched for anything that struck a familiar note. A couple of hours dragged by without any positive results. Skeeter's eyes were getting tired from staring at the screen, so she got up and went into Buck's small kitchen to fix them some sandwiches. Peanut butter and jelly seemed to be about the only option.

As she came back into the living room carrying a plate with four sandwiches on it, Buck said excitedly, "I've got 'em!"

Skeeter put the plate on the arm of Buck's sofa and hurried over to look at the screen. The name on the account at the top of the display, was *Danby, Roy J. and Martina*. Skeeter saw a confusing array of figures underneath and tried to sort them out. After a moment, she said, "Looks like ol' Roy's not doing so good."

Buck glanced up at her. "The man has a little over two hundred thousand dollars in the bank!"

"It takes a lot of money to run a ranch the size of the Rising Star. But maybe he's just having a minor cash flow problem. Can you back up a few months?"

"Sure, now that I've got the account number, we can go back as far as you want."

Buck manipulated the keyboard and the display changed, going back to the statement from Danby's account for the previous month. "Look for large withdrawals," Skeeter said.

"What do you mean by large?"

"Oh, five thousand, anyway. And probably in round numbers, too."

As they looked over the statement from that month and then backed up several more months, it became obvious that while Roy Danby's account was dwindling, it was doing so on a consistent basis, rather than in large chunks. Skeeter frowned as Buck said, "I'm not a rancher, Skeeter, but from the pattern I see here, Danby looks like any businessman who's been suffering some financial reverses, rather than somebody who's being blackmailed."

"Who said anything about blackmail?"

Buck shrugged. "That's the only thing that makes sense, the only reason you'd want to break into Danby's records and look for big hunks of cash missing."

"Well, you're right. I wanted to find out if he'd withdrawn any suspicious amounts during the last few weeks. Obviously, he hasn't, so Brannon and Turner haven't made their move yet. I can still trip them up."

"We'd better cross-check and see if there are any subsidiary accounts, hadn't we?"

"Sure, go ahead. But I don't think you'll find anything."

A few moments later, Buck said, "How about a personal

account under the name of Martina Danby?"

Skeeter leaned over his shoulder. "I haven't heard anything about Martina working. Maybe she's got money of her own, or Danby puts a certain percentage of the ranch's money in there. How's it look?"

"Check out the withdrawals."

Skeeter had to wait until he pointed out the pertinent numbers on the screen, but then she saw the same rough pattern emerging as he called up each of Martina's statements for the past year.

"She took out five hundred dollars a month starting out," Buck said. "Then it went to a couple of times a month, then a thousand twice a month. The last three months it's been twenty-five hundred, twice a month."

"Over twenty thousand dollars in the last year," Skeeter mused. "That's not so much, but it was enough to drain most of the funds in the account. A woman like Martina could probably spend that much on clothes, though."

"But if her husband is having trouble, he wouldn't be able to replace what she was spending. Maybe she didn't tell him she was spending it?"

"Maybe not. One thing we haven't considered—Danby's probably been making quite a bit of money off those dogfights. I know he was getting a percentage of Raider's winnings, and surely he has other dogs that would win some, too. That money would be cash, and it might not ever show up on bank records."

"Or IRS records."

Skeeter smiled. "That's right. He'd have a big stake in making sure Brannon and Turner keep their mouths shut. Not only would the local authorities be after him for illegal gambling and running a dogfight, but the IRS boys would want a piece of him, too."

"Sounds like these crooked cops picked a good target."

"A real good one."

"And you're going to bring the whole bunch down."

"I'm going to try," Skeeter said.

After they'd eaten, Buck called his office to confirm that he wouldn't be returning that afternoon, then changed from his suit into jeans and boots and Western shirt. "That feels a lot better," he said as he emerged from his bedroom snapping the shirt. "What now?"

"We go back by the Horsehead and see if Jasper's changed his mind about coming along."

Jasper's refusal to be part of the plan had surprised Skeeter. When she had called him over to the booth where she was sitting with Harkness and outlined what she intended to do, he had shaken his head and muttered something about damn-fool stunt.

"Don't forget the cops think maybe I helped you kill Hobson," he'd reminded her. "I want you cleared almost as bad as you do. But I don't cotton to all this stuff you're talkin' about. Sounds too dangerous."

"There's nothing dangerous about it," Skeeter had insisted, but Jasper still shook his head.

"You said them two fellas tried to kill you tonight—"

"I said they ran me off the road to scare me."

"But they'd've been mighty pleased if you'd died when your pickup went off the road. You said they admitted as much. It ain't smart to fool with fellas like that. I *know*, Skeeter."

She had wondered what he meant by that, but it had been his last word on the subject.

Now she and Buck drove on down to the Stockyards, Buck in his compact Dodge pickup, Skeeter in her full-size Ford.

The Horsehead wasn't open yet, but the front door was un-locked. Skeeter squinted a little as she pushed through the door, going from bright sunlight to the shadowy interior of the club. The place was even dimmer than usual with the neon beer signs behind the bar turned off.

"Hey, Jasper!" Skeeter called as Buck came in behind her. "Anybody home?"

The door to the storeroom stood open. Jasper emerged a second later. "Back here countin' cases of booze," he said. "Wouldn't want to run out." He put his hands on the bar and leaned on the palms. "You two playin' private eye?"

Skeeter's temper bubbled up. "Dammit, Jasper Lowe," she exclaimed, "I'm not playing a damn thing! I *am* a private investigator, and you know it!"

"Yeah, you just never brought that part of your life into my club before."

Buck moved up beside Skeeter with a slightly nervous ex-pression on his face. "Uh, maybe I'd better mosey along someplace else for a while . . ."

"No need for that, Buck," Skeeter said tightly. "Mr. Lowe and I are simply having a discussion. It just *sounded* like an ar-gument."

"I ain't arguin' with nobody," Jasper said. "Like I told you last night, Skeeter, I want this mess cleaned up. I just wish it was the cops takin' the chances, not you."

"You really think the cops are going to bust their chops to find Hobson's killer when they've got me for the part?"

"Reckon not." Jasper sighed. "Look, I know you're right. But that don't mean I have to like it, and it don't mean I've got to go along and be part of it."

Skeeter took a deep breath and said quietly, "I thought you were my friend, Jasper."

"I am. But this business has messed things up a mite."

Skeeter winced. Other than the fact that both men were quiet-spoken, Jasper and her ex-husband Will were nothing alike. But as she listened to Jasper, her memory turned back to Will and the night he had told her that even though he loved her, he couldn't stay married to her anymore. Pain flared up inside her. She'd never been one for assigning blame whenever anything bad happened, but she knew she carried her share of guilt for that break-up. She'd never been easy to live with, she knew that. But she'd always thought there would be a chance to work things out later.

That chance had never materialized, and she didn't know if she and Jasper would work things out, either. She wasn't in love with him, not like she'd been with Will, and all she and Jasper had to jeopardize was a working relationship, not a family, but she realized she didn't want to lose that.

"Jasper . . . I'm sorry."

He nodded slowly, and his voice was a little softer as he said, "Sure. We'll talk about it some other time, when all this is over."

"Yeah. We'll do that."

But Skeeter wasn't sure that time would ever come. You meant to take care of the things that were really important, but life has a way of getting in the way. Nobody had time to do it all, and there were no guarantees that tomorrow would come. So you grinned and admitted somewhere deep inside that, yeah, life was a bad deal, but you were going to do the best you could anyway. And when the good times did show up, you damn well appreciated them—because you knew they wouldn't last.

"So long, Jasper."

"Yeah. So long."

She walked out of the club with Buck tagging along beside her. "What do we do next?"

Skeeter grinned at him and said, "We go get ready to catch us some bad guys."

The cleaning crew had gone by the agency and gotten the spare house key she'd left with Lars Gilford, Skeeter saw as she opened the door. The walls had been washed, and everything in the living room was back in its place as much as possible. The damaged furniture had been taken away for repair. The same was true in the rest of the house. When she looked around, Skeeter could see plenty of reminders that Frank Hobson had been here and trashed the place, but overall the improvement was tremendous.

They'd gone by the agency and picked up the surveillance equipment Lars Gilford had gotten for them. Skeeter carried the box containing the tiny microphone/transmitter and its battery pack, while Buck had the receiver. "You sure this stuff will work?" he asked.

"It'd better," Skeeter replied. "The transmitter's supposed to have an effective range of a mile and a half, so Harkness shouldn't have any problems hearing what's going on at the ranch."

"Harkness and *me*," Buck said.

"Yeah, I know he said you could come along, but he also said you have to stay out of the way if there's any trouble. Don't you forget that."

He grinned. "Don't worry, I won't." Skeeter wasn't convinced he meant it. Harkness might've let himself in for more than he bargained for when he agreed to let Buck accompany him.

Harkness was an unusual cop, though, otherwise he'd never be helping her like this in the first place.

Skeeter unpacked the gear and looked at the microphone, which was connected to the batteries by a flexible, plastic-coated wire. Buck studied it with interest and asked, "You ever used one of those doohickeys before?"

"Doohickeys? What kind of terminology is that from a computer expert?"

"I know computers, but not this sort of stuff. This is all new to me."

"Well, to answer your question, I've never used one of these, no. But I've seen them demonstrated. Luckily, we've got time for a field test once Harkness gets here. Until then, I'd better see about putting all this get-up on the right way."

"Need any help?"

"Why, Buck Ngyuen!" she exclaimed in mock outrage. "You know I have to wear this thing under my shirt."

He looked so embarrassed as he mumbled, "Oh, yeah, I forgot," that Skeeter felt a little bad about teasing him.

"Actually," she said, "I will need some help with the tape." She reached for the snaps on her shirtfront and popped open the top one. "Think you can get the adhesive tape from the medicine cabinet in the bathroom?"

Buck blushed even more. "Uh, sure." He hurried out of the room but stuck his head back in just as Skeeter was slipping the shirt off her shoulders. "I, uh, don't reckon I know where the bathroom is."

Skeeter pointed down the hall. Buck was carefully avoiding looking at her breasts in their white bra. He was taking this a lot more seriously than Skeeter was—she had plenty of things to worry about that were a lot more important than her boobs, she thought—but she didn't want to make him uncomfortable, either. She supposed she should have waited and let Harkness help her, but she was anxious to get started and wanted to be ready to test the unit as soon as he arrived.

With a roll of adhesive tape in his hand, Buck came back

from the bathroom and asked, "Is this what you meant?"

"That's right," Skeeter said. "Bring it over here."

She took the tape from him and tore off a couple of strips, then used them to fasten the microphone to her skin just under her right breast. That would probably be far enough over to diminish the sound of her heartbeat on the pick-up, but they wouldn't know for sure until they tested the thing. They could always adjust it later. The flat little battery pack went into the small of her back. With the shirt bloused up a little back there, it would conceal any telltale bulges. She needed Buck's help for this part, standing very still as he taped the unit in place and then taped down the trailing wire. "That's it," he said when he was done. He sounded relieved.

"Thanks, Buck," she said as she reached for her shirt again. "Hope it didn't bother you too much."

"Oh, no," he said quickly. "No bother, no bother at all."

"I know it was a little awkward—"

"Oh, no."

Skeeter turned to face him as she snapped up the shirt. "What's wrong, Buck? If you're worried about seeing me with my shirt off, don't. You ain't the first to do that by a long shot, son."

He took a deep breath. "Skeeter, you have to understand. Even though I . . . I was raised primarily as an American, I was still taught to be respectful to—"

"You tell me you were raised to be respectful to your elders and I'm liable to punch you." A broad grin took any sting out of the words.

"I was going to say I was taught to be respectful to women."

"Nothing particularly Oriental about that. A few American men are respectful to women, too."

"Yes, I know. Hopalong was always a perfect gentleman,

and Roy never said a harsh word to Dale less'n she was playing a spoiled brat who thought she could catch the bad guys better than him and the Sons of the Pioneers. But you understand what I mean."

"Yeah, I think so. It's bothering you that you saw me like that."

He shook his head. "No. What's bothering me is that I want to do this." And with that, he put his hands on her shoulders and brought her up against him and kissed her.

It was a mighty nice kiss, too, and Skeeter put her arms around him without really thinking about it, hugging him tightly. When he finally took his mouth away from hers, she leaned her head against his shoulder and took a couple of deep breaths before she said, "Whoa, son."

Instantly, he sprang back a couple of feet away from her. "I'm sorry," he said. "I shouldn't have—"

She caught his arm and shook her head. "No, Buck. Don't apologize for kissing me. Shoot, there's nothing wrong with that. Nice as it'd be to take it even farther, you and me both know there's not much future in it. I'm ten years older than you, for one thing."

"That's not so much," he said.

"It seems like a lot to me," she told him gently. "Besides, I've got a couple of kids and an ex-husband and more miles on me than I like to think about. You're a nice fella . . . a heck of a nice fella . . . but I just don't know if it's right between you and me."

Buck sighed, then nodded slowly. "Reckon you're right, ma'am. You're . . . you're sort of like Miss Kitty on *Gunsmoke*. Yeah, and I'm like Thad." He grinned as it all began to make sense to him. "There couldn't ever be anything like that between us, because you've got Matt—I mean Jasper."

"Now, wait just a minute—"

"And I may be just a supporting player, but I serve my purpose, too. Yep, I can see it all now, you and Jasper are just like Miss Kitty and Matt, and I guess that makes Chuckie like Festus, except he's awfully big to be Festus and we don't have a Doc or a Newly or a Quint . . ."

Somebody knocked on the door, and Skeeter went to answer it in a hurry. Harkness stood there, wearing jeans and a knit shirt. He said, "I think I'm a little early—"

"Not hardly," Skeeter said. "Come on in before he gets to Louie the drunk."

Chapter Twenty

The equipment worked fine when they checked it out. Harkness took the battery-powered receiver and drove a good mile and a half away, then listened as Skeeter and Buck talked in normal tones of voice. When Harkness got back, he was smiling.

"Came in clear as a bell," he told them.

"What about the heartbeat?"

"It's there, but not so loud as to be a distraction. We should be able to hear everything that goes on in that ranch house—unless Danby has it shielded against transmissions."

"Which is mighty doubtful," Skeeter said. "He's just a rancher who got mixed up in some shady dealings, not some sort of spy."

"That's right, but he can still be dangerous, and so can Brannon and Turner if you're right about them."

"I am," Skeeter said grimly.

"Are you going to be carrying a gun?"

She shook her head. "I want to do everything legal-like. Since I'm officially on vacation from the agency, I think I'd better not carry."

"Well, I was prepared to look the other way if you were planning to, but I suppose you're right." Harkness glanced over at Buck. "What about you?"

"You askin' if I'm packin' a hogleg?"

"Well, yes, I think so."

Buck shook his head. "Nope. Never did cotton much to shootin' irons."

"Unh-hunh, right." Harkness looked at his watch. "We've got time to pick up something to eat before we go if anybody's hungry."

Skeeter didn't really feel much like eating—she was too nervous for that—but the evening could turn out to be a long one. "That's a good idea," she said.

They took her pickup and Harkness's Olds. Buck rode with her. The pancake house a few blocks away beside the interstate served a good chicken-fried steak in addition to the usual stacks of assorted flapjacks, so they stopped there. Skeeter didn't really taste the food, and from the way Harkness was picking at his plate, she suspected he felt the same way. Buck put away enough for all three of them. "I tend to eat when I get a little edgy," he told them.

When they were finished with the meal, they headed toward Denton. The highway to Decatur veered off to the northwest within a few miles.

This was it, Skeeter thought, glancing at the line of red on the western horizon that marked the spot where the sun had gone down earlier. They were really going through with it. By the time the night was over, she might have one set of worries taken off her head.

On the other hand, things could always get worse.

Estimating where the main house of the Rising Star Ranch was located, Skeeter figured that the spot where Harkness's car was parked in the thick shadows of a clump of oaks beside the highway was just over three-quarters of a mile in a straight line from the house. They wouldn't be very noticeable, but they would still be able to reach the ranch house in a matter of two or three minutes if there was trouble.

Of course, Skeeter thought as she drove the pickup over the cattleguard between the pillars of the gate at the ranch entrance, two or three minutes could be a long time if somebody was trying to kill you. In that case, she'd have to do whatever she could to stay alive until the cavalry—as Buck had started referring to Harkness and himself—arrived.

The house was brightly lit, she saw as she approached. Floodlights on the building itself and in the trees around it furnished enough illumination to give the illusion of day. Half a dozen cars were parked along the driveway, and again, they were fancy enough to make her pickup with its crumpled fender look especially shabby. As the truck's headlights swept over the other vehicles, she looked for the car Brannon and Turned had used to run her off the road the night before. She didn't spot it, which was no surprise. They'd probably turned it in and drawn a new one. She did see a large luxury sedan that looked vaguely familiar, but she wasn't sure if she had really seen it before or not. All big fancy cars tended to look alike to her.

She parked at the end of the line and got out. She was wearing the fringed and beaded denim jacket, along with a pair of tight jeans and a white shirt. The jacket would help cover up the battery pack, and since she wore it open in the front, it wouldn't muffle the reception from the microphone. She might not be as rich as these people here tonight, Skeeter thought as she walked toward the door, but she looked damn good anyway.

The gate onto the patio was open, and the courtyard was lit up, too. Even though the front door was closed, Skeeter could hear music coming from inside. She grimaced a little. Loud music would probably overwhelm any conversation being transmitted. She'd have to get Brannon and Turner into some quieter place before she maneuvered them into incriminating themselves.

A Mexican maid in a starched white outfit answered the

door about thirty seconds after Skeeter pressed the button beside it. Skeeter smiled and said, "Howdy. I'm Skeeter Shively, and Mr. and Mrs. Danby invited me to drop by tonight."

"*Si, senorita,* please come in."

Skeeter stepped into the foyer and the maid closed the door. The music was even louder in here, and as much as Skeeter liked Willie and Waylon, the sound was a little overpowering. The maid had to raise her voice to ask if Skeeter wanted her to take her purse or jacket. Skeeter shook her head no to both questions. She especially wanted to hang onto her purse.

She wasn't carrying a gun, that much was true. But she hadn't said anything to Harkness about the rolls of pennies in the bottom of her purse. They gave the bag enough weight to make it a surprisingly effective weapon, and she'd also been known to wrap her fingers around a roll of coins when she was about to punch somebody, too. Came in handy at the Horsehead from time to time.

There were about a dozen people in the living room when Skeeter sauntered in. She looked them over without being too obvious about it. Everybody was drinking and talking and having a fine old time. She spotted Roy and Martina Danby talking to a tall, slender man who had his back to her. The Danbys shifted slightly and so did their companion, and Skeeter saw that he was Crispin Loomis.

Her spine stiffened a little, but she kept the smile on her face as Roy Danby noticed her and started toward her, bringing his wife and Loomis with him. Her brain was screaming curses. She forced herself to stay calm and glance at Loomis with the vague curiosity of somebody who had never seen the other person before. For his part, Loomis seemed to be doing the same thing, and Skeeter felt a surge of hope that he wouldn't give away her real identity.

"Skeeter!" Roy Danby said over the blasting music. "I was hoping you'd make it! There's somebody here I want you to meet. Skeeter Shively, this is Crispin Loomis. Cris, this little lady is Skeeter Shively. She's new in the dog-breeding game."

Loomis put out his hand and Skeeter took it. For some reason of his own, Loomis was playing along with her charade, because he said, "Very pleased to meet you, Ms. Shively. When Roy here told me he knew a lady who might be interested in selling me some dogs, I didn't expect her to be such a lovely young woman."

"Well, thank you, Mr. Loomis. I'm looking forward to talking business with you."

"Certainly." Loomis sipped his drink. "This evening is for pleasure, however. What did you call it, Roy? A get-acquainted party?"

"That's right," Danby said, slapping Loomis on the shoulder. The Englishman flinched a little from the hearty gesture, but Danby didn't seem to notice. "Cris and I have a lot of mutual friends, but tonight's the first time we've met face to face. Hell, I feel like we're already old pards."

What Danby was feeling was greed, Skeeter thought. With his ranch having trouble, he probably looked on Loomis as a new source of income, a new sucker. She wondered how many of the other guests here tonight fell into that category. She recognized a few of them from the dogfight, but most of them she had never seen before. They were being recruited, she realized, brought into the inner circle to furnish more dogs, more bets, more illicit money for Roy Danby.

But where the hell were Brannon and Turner? Everything would be ruined if they weren't here, too.

For the moment, all she could do was wait. When Martina asked her if she'd like a drink, she nodded and said, "Please."

"How about a margarita?"

"That'd be just dandy."

Martina looked smashing in a white jacket and a long burgundy dress that clung to the curves of her slender body. She mixed the drink herself and brought it to Skeeter, who said sincerely, "Thanks."

"Go ahead and mingle and enjoy yourself," Martina told her with a smile. "I think you'll be able to make some valuable contacts here this evening."

"I hope so."

What she hoped was that none of these people knew much more about dog breeding than she did—not much at all, in other words. She didn't want to get caught in some obvious mistake.

She found herself talking to a white-haired, distinguished-looking doctor from Fort Worth. The man had his elegant blonde wife on his arm, and as Skeeter talked to them, she wondered why in the world people like this would want to get mixed up in something as sordid as dogfighting.

She thought she heard the sound of the doorbell over the music and looked toward the foyer in time to see the maid letting in Brannon and Turner. They were wearing Western suits tonight and looked as smooth and slick and well-to-do as anybody else in the room. Danby probably thought of them as new blood, too, unaware that they were the ones who planned to do the bleeding. She watched Danby greet them effusively, pumping their hands and ushering them toward the bar. Skeeter managed to keep the husky doctor and his wife between her and the two cops so they wouldn't see her just yet.

The music stopped, and the abrupt silence seemed almost louder. Skeeter realized the CD had come to an end, but after a few seconds, the player in the elaborate stereo system started on another one, this time Jerry Jeff Walker. As the poignant lyrics of "Desperadoes Waitin' for a Train" filled the room, she excused herself from the doctor and his wife and started drifting toward Brannon and Turner. Danby was introducing them to Crispin Loomis, she saw, and as she approached, the rancher moved on. Skeeter stepped up behind Brannon and said, "Howdy, boys."

Brannon jumped a little at the sound of her voice and jerked his head around. Turner did the same thing. As they stared at her, Brannon growled, "What the hell are you doing here?"

Skeeter's fingers tightened on the stem of the margarita glass she held. A part of her wanted to shatter it and rake the jagged edges across Brannon's face. She forced that impulse down and said, "I'm like you two. I came to talk business."

"I take it the three of you know each other?" Loomis asked coolly.

"They know who I really am," Skeeter told him, "just like you. But I know some things that none of you do."

"Like what?" Turner asked, his voice tight with anger.

"Like who killed Frank Hobson."

Brannon snorted in contempt. "That's easy. The cops think you did."

"No. I mean I know who really killed him."

And just like that, she did. The words had been meant as a bluff, an attempt to force Brannon and Turner out of the room and into some place where Harkness could hear them confess to planning to blackmail Roy Danby. But suddenly things started clicking into place in Skeeter's mind, and every instinct in her body was screaming the identity of the killer.

But that was all it was—instinct. She didn't have a bit of proof.

"I don't know what you're talking about," Brannon said,

"but I don't want you causing trouble. Why don't we take a walk outside?"

"I was just about to suggest the same thing," Loomis said. "I was under the impression you gentlemen were dog fanciers, but I see now I must have been wrong." The gambler's free hand was hovering near the opening of his coat, and Skeeter wondered if he had a gun under there.

It was a likely enough proposition to be worrisome to Brannon and Turner, who had to be armed, too. Turner said, "Come on. I want to get this straightened out." He forced a grin for Loomis. "I still think we can do some business."

"One can only hope."

If they expected Skeeter to give them trouble, they were disappointed, because she nodded toward a door in the rear of the room that opened onto another patio. The Spanish-style house was probably built around a series of such courtyards, she realized.

As she started toward the door along with the three men, she wondered how much of the conversation Harkness and Buck had been able to overhear. Loomis, Brannon, and Turner had all kept their voices pitched low, so that they couldn't be heard over the music by the other people in the room. Once they got outside, Skeeter thought, the reception would probably be a lot better.

She wasn't being the complete fool that the others probably thought her. The crooked cops might figure they could knock her out, slip her away from the house, and kill her, and there was no telling what was in Loomis's mind. Given his reputation, he was probably waiting to see what was going to happen before he cast his lot. Skeeter felt fairly confident that he wouldn't stop at murder if he thought it was in his best interests.

Brannon had his hand on her arm in what looked like a

friendly fashion. Skeeter waited until they were almost to the door, then suddenly pulled loose and stepped over beside Roy Danby, who was holding court along with his wife in front of the fireplace. Danby gave her a puzzled glance as she said, "Could we tear you and Martina away for a few minutes, Roy?" She nodded toward Brannon, Turner, and Loomis, who was standing tensely by the door. "We need to talk a little business."

"Well, Skeeter, I'd be glad to, but don't you think it'd be better to wait—"

She didn't let him finish. "No, I'm afraid not. I know I'm not being a very polite guest, but I really need your input on this deal, Roy."

"Well, in that case . . ." He put his empty drink glass on the mantel. "Come on, Martina. We've got to go see some men about a dog, I suppose."

Chuckling at his own joke, he took his wife's hand and followed Skeeter over to the door. Loomis opened it and they all filed out.

Danby immediately became more serious when the door was shut behind them and they were standing on the flagstones of the small patio, which was dimly lit by a couple of small lanterns in fruit trees that had already lost most of their leaves. His breath plumed a little in the chilly air as he said, "Look, I don't want to be inhospitable, gentlemen, but this was supposed to be a social gathering. Business can come later."

"Evidently it can't," Loomis said. "At least according to Ms. Barlow here."

Danby and Martina both frowned. "Barlow?" Danby echoed. He looked at Skeeter. "I thought your name was Shively."

"She's Skeeter Barlow," Brannon snapped. "She's a private detective from Fort Worth. Whatever else she's told you is a bunch of bullshit."

Danby's mouth tightened into an angry line. "A private detective?" he said. "What the hell's going on here?"

Skeeter smiled and nodded toward Brannon and Turner. "Ask them. They're cops."

Martina gasped, "Cops?"

"Vice cops, to be precise. They're working for a task force on illegal gambling—including dogfights."

Danby turned sharply to face the two officers, his fists clenched. "Dammit, is this true?" he demanded.

Turner, the more nervous of the two, slipped a short-barreled revolver from under his coat. He didn't point it at Danby, but he held it ready. Brannon stayed cool and said, "Take it easy, Danby. You'd have found out soon anyway."

"Then it is true? I offer you the hospitality of my home and you betray me?"

"We haven't betrayed anybody. There's nothing for you to worry about."

"Not as long as you give us what we want," Turner added.

"Son . . . of . . . a . . . bitch!" Danby said. "You guys are trying to blackmail me!"

Brannon shrugged. "Yeah, I guess you could say that."

Well, this was working out all right so far, Skeeter thought. She hoped Harkness and Buck were getting an earful. A muscle twitched in her cheek, but she forced herself to relax. Her nerves were stretched so tight that if she let go of them, she'd probably have a hissy fit. And she couldn't afford that right now.

Danby swung toward Loomis. "What about you? What's your part in this?"

"Interested bystander? I don't really have a part, old boy. I'm here because we had a mutual friend in the late Frank

Hobson and because I thought you and I might be able to place a few wagers between ourselves and your other friends. All of this about cops and private eyes is news to me, although I was aware that Ms. Shively here was really Ms. Barlow. We met when the late Mr. Hobson was trying to kill her."

"Yeah, and she killed Hobson," Brannon said, "but that doesn't have anything to do with anything else, Roy."

Danby looked at Skeeter again. "*You* killed Frank?"

She shook her head. "No, I didn't."

"But *he* was trying to kill you?"

"Because he thought one of my clients cut Raider's throat and he blamed me for it."

"Raider? The dog?"

"Yeah. It's sort of a long story."

"I don't give a damn how long it is," Danby said. "I want this mess straightened up—" He glanced at Brannon and Turner. "—whatever it takes."

"Our feelings exactly," Brannon agreed.

Turner said, "Yeah."

Skeeter said, "They didn't want me telling you that they were cops until they were good and ready to hit you for black-mail money. I guess they don't know how much trouble you've been having with the ranch, Roy. Unless things improve, they're not going to be able to take you for much."

"Shut up," Brannon said tiredly. "This doesn't have anything to do with you anymore, Barlow."

Danby was staring at her again. "How . . . how the hell did you know the ranch was having trouble?"

Skeeter summoned up one last smile and said, "I know a lot more than that, Roy. I know—"

She was about to say that she knew who killed Frank Hobson when several screams from inside the house made all of them turn and look in that direction. Through the glass in

201

the upper half of the door, they saw the other guests scurrying out of the way of a woman who stalked wild-eyed through the room, her head jerking from side to side as she looked around for something. She spotted the group of people standing in the courtyard and came toward them, throwing the door open and stepping out into the night.

"There you are!" Laurie Hobson cried. She lifted the gun in her hand and pointed it toward Martina Danby. "I've been looking for you, slut!"

Oh, damn, Skeeter thought as her heart tried to bounce right out of her chest. Looked like Harkness and Buck were about to overhear a lot more than any of them had expected.

Chapter Twenty-one

Over Laurie's harsh breathing, Skeeter could hear the sounds of car doors slamming, motors starting, and wheels spinning on gravel. A crazy woman waving a gun around tended to clear out a party pretty fast.

Turner lifted the pistol and called out, "Police officers! Drop the gun!"

Laurie didn't budge. She had her sights lined on Martina, and when Skeeter glanced in her direction, she saw that Martina was standing there motionless, eyes wide with fear. She said, "I . . . I don't even know you . . ."

"You ought to know me, slut. You've been screwing my husband." Laurie reached into the pocket of her jeans with her free hand and pulled out a photograph. "I found this when I was going through Frank's things, and a lot more like it! You and that no good jerk must've had a lot of fun, laughing at me!"

"I swear, we didn't—"

"Shut up! It's too late for excuses!"

Brannon said, "You'd better put that gun down, ma'am. My partner and I really are police officers."

"This doesn't have anything to do with the rest of you," Laurie said. "It's between me and her. She stole my husband."

Where the heck were Harkness and Buck? Until help showed up, she wanted to keep Laurie from going over the edge and pulling the trigger.

"Wait a minute, Laurie," Skeeter said sharply. "Remember me?"

Laurie didn't tear her eyes away from Martina. But she said, "Yeah. The woman with the dogs."

"I don't have any reason to lie to you, Laurie, so you know this is the truth. Frank wasn't in love with Martina, not ever."

"What are you talking about?" Laurie's voice rose shrilly. "I've got the pictures—"

"You've got pictures of them having sex, but that's all. And the only reason Frank did it was so that he could blackmail Martina."

Martina didn't say anything, but Danby exclaimed, "You're crazy! Martina would never cheat on me. Those pictures you're talking about must be fakes!"

Skeeter shook her head. "Sorry, Roy, but they're not. Witnesses saw Martina visiting Frank Hobson plenty of times while Laurie was at work. But all Hobson really wanted was her money, so that he could pay off Loomis."

Danby swung back toward the Englishman. "Hobson owed you money?"

"A great deal," Loomis confirmed. "When you and your associate Mr. Wade took over ownership of Hobson's dog, he found it very difficult to pay me what he owed. I can imagine him turning to blackmail."

"Because he knew you'd have your boys kill him if he didn't come up with the cash," Skeeter said.

Loomis just shrugged.

Brannon said, "This is interesting as all hell, but it still doesn't have anything to do with why we're here tonight, Roy. Turner and I can square all of this for you and put things back to normal—for a price."

Skeeter didn't give Danby a chance to respond. She said to Brannon, "He can't pay you. Just like Martina couldn't keep paying Hobson. That's what she told him when he came up here to see her Monday night."

"Hobson was *here?*" Danby asked.

Skeeter glanced at Martina, whose eyes were still fixed on the barrel of Laurie's pistol. Evidently Martina wasn't going to tell the story, so Skeeter thought she might as well. "He was here," she said. "After he jumped me at the Horsehead and Loomis's boys ran him off, he finally calmed down and realized that revenge was one thing but survival was another. And he wasn't going to survive unless he came up with some money for Loomis. So he came to see Martina and told her she had to pay him again to keep him from telling you about their affair. There was no money left, though. He'd already bled her personal account dry. She may have siphoned off some of the ranch's profits, too, Roy; you'll have to check on that. But when she told Hobson there wouldn't be any more money, he left mad, probably saying that he was going to send you those pictures of him and Martina."

They were all listening to her now as she pieced together the theory that had come to her earlier in the evening. A lot of it was guesswork and instinct, but it fit the facts. Skeeter took a deep breath. "Hobson went back to Fort Worth. What he didn't know was that Martina had followed him. He drove to my house and parked, and she pulled up behind him. I don't know what she told him—probably that she had changed her mind and brought him some cash. He sat there in his truck while she reached into her purse and pulled out a gun and put it against his head and fired."

The barrel of Laurie's gun began to wobble as the impact of Skeeter's words sunk in. "You mean . . . *she* killed Frank? After all I did to try to get him back . . . after I risked my life killing that damned dog of his . . . she just took him away forever?"

Skeeter still didn't understand why either one of these women would have wanted a loser like Hobson. She said,

"That's right. She killed Frank. Didn't you, Martina?"

Martina's face finally showed some emotion again. Her lips curved in a slight smile as she said, "Yes, I did. I was just so *tired* of him."

Laurie screamed, "Damn you!" Her finger jerked the trigger of the gun.

The bullet screamed off into the night sky. Turner had fired a split-second before she did, shooting her twice in the chest. The bullets knocked Laurie backward against the door into the house.

Skeeter was moving even as the gunshots racketed through the air. She threw herself toward Martina, pulling her to the ground just in case Turner missed. As soon as Martina was down, Skeeter rolled to the side and came up on her feet, swinging her purse at the full extension of its straps. The load of rolled pennies cracked against the side of Turner's head.

The crooked cop staggered. Skeeter leaped past him. Brannon made a grab for her, but he was too late. Skeeter headed for another of those wrought-iron gates she had spotted on the other side of the patio. She hoped it wasn't locked.

It wasn't. She slapped up the latch and knocked the gate open with her shoulder as a gun blasted behind her and a bullet whined off the iron grillwork. Then she was running out in the open, leaving the house behind her. Over the hammering of her pulse in her head, she heard Brannon shout, "Stop her, dammit!"

She wished there'd been a chance to get to Laurie's gun, but there had been too many people between her and it. She circled around the back of the house, fear giving her the speed she thought she'd lost in the years since high school track meets. Brannon and Turner would kill her if they caught her, she knew that. They thought they could still cover up every-thing that had happened tonight and continue to blackmail Danby, just as they had planned. Only now they had even more ammunition, since Martina had confessed to murder.

Gasping for air, Skeeter headed down the hill toward the building where the dogfights had taken place. She heard guns going off again behind her, but if they were shooting at her, the bullets weren't coming close enough for her to hear them. What the devil had happened to Harkness and Buck? Couldn't they tell there was a small-scale war going on out here?

As she reached the building and leaned against the wall for a few seconds, trying to catch her breath, she heard the dogs growling inside, no doubt disturbed by all the shooting. Fair enough; she was pretty damn disturbed, too. She started around the building.

"There she is!"

That was Martina's voice, Skeeter realized. So she'd joined the hunt. Well, that was to be expected. She had a big stake in this. After all, she was a murderer.

Skeeter thought about trying to get inside the building and turn the dogs loose. That would certainly cause some confu-sion if she could do it. But the animals would be just as likely to tear into her as they would the others, and besides, she didn't want to get herself cornered inside. Better to head for the highway, she decided. She darted from the building to the shadows of the trees surrounding it. When she glanced toward the house, she could see her pickup still parked up there at the top of the hill. Too far away, too many guns be-tween her and it, she thought with a grimace.

"Stop, Skeeter."

Martina again, a lot closer this time. Too close. She moved quietly for a rich lady, Skeeter thought disgustedly.

Martina loomed out of the night, no more than fifteen feet from her, and she held a rifle in her hands. Skeeter didn't move as Martina approached.

"I was hoping it would be a pleasant evening," Martina said with a sigh.

"Things don't always work out the way we hope."

"No, they don't, do they?" Without taking her eyes off Skeeter, Martina called softly, "We're over here, Roy."

As Danby came around the corner of the building and walked toward her, also carrying a rifle, Skeeter said, "What are you going to do?"

"Well, I'm afraid we'll have to kill you. That's the only thing that makes any sense. This is a big ranch. We'll find a nice place to put you and that Hobson woman. I'm sorry, Skeeter. Roy and I are just trying to hang on."

"Brannon and Turner will bleed you dry."

"They'll try." Martina laughed quietly. "Like I said, it's a big ranch."

She meant there was plenty of room for hidden graves, Skeeter realized. "Going to just kill everybody who knows anything about this, are you? Loomis, too?"

"If we have to."

Danby walked up beside his wife. The moonlight was bright enough for Skeeter to see that the gun in his hands was one of the Winchesters she had admired on the wall of their living room. Martina held the other one.

Skeeter gestured at the rifles. "Those the real thing?"

"Of course," Martina said. "We wouldn't waste our money on fakes. They're in excellent working condition, too."

There was something wrong with Danby's breathing. It was harsh and ragged, and his features were contorted. Skeeter heard yelling and looked up the hill and saw three figures running toward them. Brannon, Turner, and Loomis. They were shouting and waving their arms, and Skeeter suddenly heard the sound of a racing engine. Headlights speared through the darkness as a vehicle topped one of the rises.

The cavalry was finally on its way.

But maybe too late, Skeeter thought grimly.

Martina said urgently, "Go ahead and kill her, Roy. We'll put the other rifle in her hands and make it look like self-defense. Brannon and Turner will back us up, and we can deal with them later."

Danby moved to the side, putting a few feet between him and Martina. In a choked voice, he said, "Frank, Martina? You cheated on me with somebody like *Frank Hobson?*"

"Roy, there's not enough time—"

Danby turned and fired, jacked the lever of the Winchester and fired again. The bullets punched through Martina's body, making her shudder as she dropped the rifle in her hands. She crumpled to the ground.

Skeeter stayed where she was. If she tried to make a dive for the fallen gun, Danby could easily blast her. He could anyway, but maybe he wouldn't if she didn't move. Wouldn't be much point in it now, Skeeter realized.

He didn't even look at her. He turned and ran toward Brannon and Turner and Loomis, shouting curses and firing the rifle from the hip. The other three men scattered, muzzle flashes winking in the night as they returned fire. Skeeter dropped to the ground to present a smaller target, then crawled forward and grabbed the Winchester Martina had dropped. She watched as a slug found Danby, jerking him back a step. He staggered ahead again, but only for a second. Then he pitched forward onto his face and didn't move.

The van screeched to a stop—*Van?* That was Jasper's van, Skeeter realized suddenly. What the hell was Jasper doing out here? But there was no time to wonder about that as a figure leaped out and more gunfire crackled. Skeeter sprang to her feet and ran forward, wanting to help if that was Jasper placing his life in danger for her. But as she raced up to the van, Jasper came out of it and grabbed her and jerked the rifle out of her hands. He tossed it away and hugged her tightly, and Skeeter watched over his shoulder as Harkness herded Brannon and Turner and Loomis up to the vehicle at gunpoint. There was a bloody patch on Brannon's shoulder and he was mewling in pain. Turner just looked scared to death, and Loomis wasn't his usual unflappable self.

Skeeter whispered, "Jasper, I don't know what the heck you're doing here, but I sure am glad to see you."

He patted her lightly on the back and rasped, "Yeah. Me, too."

Buck stuck his head out the window of the van and asked, "All the shootin' over?"

"Looks like it," Harkness grunted. "There's a phone in the van, Buck. Get on it and get us some help. Highway patrol, sheriff's department, any damn thing you can get."

"You bet." Buck's head disappeared from the window.

Without taking his eyes off his prisoners, Harkness said icily, "You may have gotten all of us in a heap of trouble, Ms. Barlow. I hope you're satisfied."

Skeeter grinned wearily and tightened her arms around Jasper. "It'll do for now," she said.

Chapter Twenty-two

The really surprising part of it all, was that nobody died. With all the bullets that had been flying around, with all the wounds that had been suffered, somebody should have been killed.

Laurie Hobson was in the hospital for three weeks. One of Turner's bullets had punctured a lung and the other tore up some meat and bone but missed any vital organs. She was in the courtroom for every day of Martina Danby's trial, still looking weak and washed out, but the fire of her hate kept her going.

Martina was in and out of a coma for a while, and when she finally came out of it for good, she spent a couple of months in the hospital before she was well enough to be transferred to the county jail. Her husband—who would limp the rest of his life from the bullet that had torn up his right leg and almost caused him to bleed to death—made bail for her and hired the best lawyers he could find, ignoring his own legal troubles to concentrate on hers. Folks were hard to figure out, Skeeter thought as she watched them in the courtroom.

Martina was found guilty, in the second degree, and got twenty years in prison. She'd be out in five or so, Skeeter figured. But five years behind bars would be a hell of a long time to a woman like Martina Danby. No pretty clothes, no fine things. Just survival.

As for Danby himself, he was sentenced to fifteen years in prison for the attempted murder of his wife and also found guilty of assorted charges involving illegal dogfights and gambling. All told, he'd probably do more time inside than Martina would. Didn't hardly seem fair, but ever since she'd been in law school, Skeeter had known that the justice system was something they called it for want of a better name.

Brannon and Turner lied up a storm about their involvement in the whole thing, but Harkness's testimony was enough to start their superiors looking into some other shady dealings. They wound up being fired from the police force and indicted for extortion and racketeering—charges on which they were both acquitted. For a while, they made noises about suing Skeeter, Harkness, the city of Fort Worth, and damn near everybody else in sight, but no suits were ever filed and the two former cops left town. Skeeter never saw either one of them again, but she read in the paper that Brannon had been killed in San Antonio, gunned down in the armed robbery of a Burger King where he was the assistant manager.

Laurie Hobson pleaded guilty to a charge of cruelty to animals in the case of Raider's death and was fined five hundred dollars. The Wise County grand jury declined to indict her on any criminal charges. Skeeter sometimes wondered if she was still working at the beauty shop in Decatur.

Lieutenant John Harkness was suspended from his job for a month—with pay—and reprimanded by his chief for his highly irregular conduct of an investigation. Behind the scenes, folks didn't seem too upset with the results he had gotten.

Crispin Loomis walked. No evidence was found to indicate that he was guilty of anything except being in the wrong place at the wrong time.

But all of that came later . . .

"You know how it is," Harkness said at the Horsehead

when they gathered there after the various law enforcement agencies involved finished questioning all of them. "Everything seems to go wrong at once. First the transmission from that mike started breaking up so badly we didn't even know you were in trouble at first, Skeeter, and then the damn car wouldn't start. That's the last time I go and buy a starter at a wrecking yard."

Buck sipped his beer and said, "Jasper showed up while the lieutenant and I were runnin' down the highway toward the gate. Mighty lucky he did."

It was long after closing time, and the volume on the jukebox had been turned down so that the ballad Willie Nelson was singing was just background music. Skeeter looked across the table at Jasper and asked, "What were you doing out there? You still haven't explained how you turned up just in the nick of time."

"Pure dumb luck." Jasper grinned ruefully. "I decided I'd been too hard on you earlier in the day, so I figured I'd better go see if I could find you and apologize. Never thought I'd run right into a shootout."

"Well, it's a good thing you did," Buck said. "Those hombres would've killed Skeeter."

She shuddered a little. "I don't want to *ever* go through anything like that again. I'm a pretty tough ol' gal, but that was too much."

Jasper took her hand. "You're tough, all right, but you ain't old."

"Better watch it." Skeeter smiled. "You're startin' to sound gallant."

Harkness leaned back in his chair and swallowed some of his beer. "You know, you'll be lucky if you don't lose your P.I. license over this, Skeeter."

"Why?" she demanded. "What'd I do wrong?"

"You didn't even have a client," he pointed out. "You engaged in some possibly illegal surveillance, and there may be charges of concealing evidence—"

"I didn't hide a damn thing! As for a client, I had a client. Anyway, it's not my fault all you cops were sittin' on your backsides."

Harkness grinned at her. "And you're luckier than you've got any legal right to be." He drained the rest of his beer. "Ah, hell, it'll all get sorted out. We're alive. I guess that's all that matters."

"Yeah," Skeeter said. "Alive and kicking. Come on, Jasper." She stood up, still holding his hand.

"What?" he asked.

"You're going to dance with me."

"I'm goin' to what?"

"Come on. Scoot them boots, cowboy. If you don't want to, I reckon Buck'd be glad to dance with a lady."

"Durned tootin', ma'am," Buck said.

Jasper sighed and followed her onto the dance floor while Buck hurried over to the jukebox, turned up the volume, and punched several of the selection buttons. The music welled up as Skeeter went into Jasper's arms. Buck and Harkness grinned and began to clap their hands and tap their toes.

And they danced the night away.